THE
SECRET
OF THE
URNS

An ABC Sci-Fi Mystery for Young Adults

A.B. CAROLAN

The Secret of the Urns

An ABC Sci-Fi Mystery for Young Adults

A.B. Carolan

ISBN: 978-1-77242-087-6

Carrick Publishing

Cover Art and Design by Sara Carrick
Production by Donna Carrick

PART I:
HARD FIST

A.B. CAROLAN

Chapter One

My leg was broken. *Way to go, girl!*

That wasn't my only worry. Kids break bones all the time. Hard Fist's climate would kill me, not the break.

There wasn't likely to be anyone near, and no one knew where I was. I didn't even know, and, even if I did, I couldn't communicate the location to anyone. Nobody within yelling distance, and even radio signals would be blocked where I lay flat on my back in pain.

Although it was still hot, the white sun had just gone down behind the precipice's edge, leaving me in shadow, except for Big Fellow's pale light dominating the twilight sky of its satellite Hard Fist. Soon night would fall, temperatures would plummet, and I would freeze.

At least the ubiquitous sounds from the satellite's rainforest had started up again to provide me with some funeral music. Of course, those sounds would make the dirge a bit primitive; some might even say they were threatening. You could almost hear chanted words to the effect, "Humans don't belong here!" *Yeah, tell my parents that!*

My usual cheery thirteen-year-old innocence and positive outlook on life had suffered a major blow along with my leg. I was thinking they'd morphed into stupidity instead. Fact is, I'm not stupid—I'm the child of a triad that had bioengineered my mental and physical attributes as well as they could, given the genetic material they had available, which was AOK considering each member of the triad had the same thing done for them. But I'd just acted stupidly, so I could almost hear old Darwin crowing about natural selection being the better choice.

So far, growing up on Hard Fist hadn't been easy. The planet-sized moon orbits the gas giant Big Fellow, almost a star itself and about twice the size of Jupiter. This largest planet in the Fistian star system lies at the E-zone's edge, so its satellite is theoretically habitable, but barely so in practice, at least for Humans. Some of my difficulties growing up there had their origin in the harsh environment. *And now it might kill me!*

Hard Fist broke all the rules. Tides were huge due to Big Fellow's proximity. When they combined with strong winds from a storm, lowlands close to the shore flooded, so communities weren't found close to the shore. Lush tropical forests took advantage of 0.9 relative to E-normal gravity and the greenhouse effect, but all that vegetation also saturated the air with free oxygen while fixing excess nitrogen. The whole atmosphere is in a strange equilibrium that scientists were just beginning to understand. Other nearby but smaller satellites toyed with Big Fellow's powerful attraction enough to keep our moon from being tide-locked to the gas giant, another precarious equilibrium, although that didn't matter much because Big Fellow wasn't a star. These were strange equilibriums that had lasted for eons, though. I'd never wanted to understand their intricacies, but we all suffered from their effects.

Even in the 21st century, Human scientists knew there were many planets in near-Earth space. Turned out many are habitable; in other words, there are many places where Humans can live. At the personal level, though, people don't have to like living in those places. For my tenure on Hard Fist, I had no choice. I couldn't leave my legal wardens, my parents, until I was eighteen—or, unless I received their permission to do so, which I'd been on the verge of asking many times recently. Because

I was often invisible to them in a manner of speaking, having a chance to ask or receive permission wasn't likely to happen anytime soon, though. I did the best I could to cope.

I had difficulties with grown-ups in general. Most of these problems could be traced to their not remembering what it was like to be a kid. They were mostly scientists, engineers, and other technical people who were sent to Hard Fist to study that strange moon. While there should have been a law against it, some of them had kids. I'm one of those. My name is Asako Kobayashi, a Human Fistian, the first one. Others followed, but I'm unique, as if that mattered. *Write that on my funeral urn, Mom and Dad2*. Of course, they might never find my body!

***

Humans had found native Fistians on Hard Fist—we didn't know how many exactly, but certainly a lot more than Humans. The Human grown-ups didn't socialize with them. The "official reason" was that they were studying native Fistians and everything else Fistian, the entire biosphere, in other words, so they didn't want to lose their objectivity.

By the time I turned ten (standard years, not Fistian years), I knew the real reason: Humans generally didn't like native Fistians. Some even expressed their prejudices openly, especially recent arrivals. Others never admitted to having them but exhibited them through their actions. Almost everyone considered the moon's natives barely sentient and primitive. I knew better.

My parents were a lot more understanding than some. They allowed me to play with Marcello, my Fistian friend. I needed that playtime because all the other Human kids were much younger, many just babies. I knew most of Marcello's clan too. I named the clan mother, the cultural and political boss, Mama Dora. She's about as ancient and tough as anyone could seem to be for a young girl of thirteen. You don't fool around with Mama Dora.

In many ways, the Fistians were more tolerant than Humans. The name Fistians came from the Human name for the moon, of course. I knew very little of their language, but I knew they called Hard Fist Mother and themselves Mother's People, or just the People. I could barely pronounce the first and gave up on the combination. It was strange that no Human scientist was studying Fistians and their language because language says a lot about culture. They didn't study the culture either.

Marcello, my best friend, is way down in the pecking order in his village and about four or five generations removed from Mama Dora as near as I could tell. Three times my size—still small compared to a grown male— he is gentle and has a great sense of humor. He'd play tricks on me, like the time he jumped out in front of me on the road coming home from school one day and made me scream.

The Fistian young don't go to our school. That never made sense to me either. They pick up languages faster than Humans, for example. While I struggled with the dead but "classic" languages English and Mandarin— ones we only see in computer history files or hear in ancient videos—Marcello spoke them fluently, as well as Standard, that mish-mash of the two languages, with lots of bits and pieces from others, that had developed among Spacers back in the home solar system.

I once saw a drawing of a centaur in a video called "Mythical Creatures of Earth"—yeah, it was in old English. Other Humans on Hard Fist used the word in a derogatory sense, so I'd become curious and queried

Einstein, the camp's AI, about it. Marcello looks a little bit like a centaur. He's harder to ride because his back slopes at a thirty degree angle from his butt up to his head—not like a horse's body at all (a few non-mythological Earth creatures had survived the Tali invasion of Earth and were taken to other near-Earth systems, so I'd seen videos of live horses).

You have to sprawl on top of Marcello and hold on to his thick mane for dear life as he gallops through the forest, pawing branches aside with those big hands and strong arms, laughing via snorts and grinning with his dancing eyebrows while I scream for him to slow down. In fact, one time he suddenly did, just to piss me off. I went sailing into a scummy pond. He stood on the bank, swishing at swamp flies with his thick tail, and bellowed out his laughter. A real comedian.

It took me a week to get the stench out of my hair. It took me two to forgive him.

***

The day I broke my leg I hadn't been able to find Marcello. A member of his clan told me he'd gone hunting in the high country. I liked the high country—it was a little cooler there in the daytime, which was nice, and much colder at night, which wasn't. I was upset that he hadn't taken me with him, so I went to find him. *Big mistake!*

There are no volcanoes on Hard Fist, but there are rivers of lava. The huge gravitational pull from Big Fellow kneads the satellite, about the size of Earth, into a wrinkled elastic ball with many cracks all over it. The thermal activity created at its core, so visible from space, more than compensates for being on the E-zone's cold edge. Add the greenhouse effect, and you have a tropical climate, except at the poles, but one with wide temperature swings between day and night.

The lava rivers don't flow like rivers, though, because the cracks in the mantle begin, wander a bit in a north-south direction, and then end. The Fistians work around them. Those rivers are especially beautiful when one terminus reaches out into the ocean, and the crack becomes an angry fjord complete with a crashing kilometers-wide waterfall where seawater turns into steam. That water vapor rises, condenses into clouds, and rains down on the lush forests filled with flora and fauna so varied that our scientists haven't even begun to catalog all the species.

Enter the drooler, the most feared predator prowling under the rainforest's tall canopy. Preying on everything from the large insect-like four-winged creatures to its own kind, alive or carrion, this fellow is a lumbering eating machine. I hadn't counted on meeting one, though. They were solitary beasts and only sociable when you look like food.

We call them droolers because they slobber as they walk. Behind all the slobbers, they have plenty of sharp teeth—that doesn't add anything to their charm. They are nasty, vile creatures that will even take on an adult Fistian to get a full meal, but they'll also eat Humans as appetizers.

Most of the time, though, droolers are slow enough that you can run away from them. That's easy to do because they smell like algae rotting in a 'ponics tank. We Humans don't have a keen sense of smell, but we can still smell a drooler about two or three klicks away. A native Fistian can pick up that odor from an even greater distance. In either case, the strategy is clear: you just make sure you move away from the drooler's stench. Other directions aren't recommended.

I figured local fauna should be able to detect a drooler's stench as well as or better than a native Fistian, so I wondered how the stinky creatures caught anything to eat. There were conjectures about them hunting in packs so their prey wouldn't have anywhere to go as the circle around them closed. Hard to say whether the conjecture had any substance because no Human had seen packs of droolers. On the contrary, they seemed like solitary beasts, so maybe fresh meat was caught by accident, and they mostly dined on carrion.

I wasn't about to go looking for droolers to find out more about them. But this one had found me.

He was a youngster, though, and moved about as fast as I did. (I say "he" because the males have bright blue-green balls that are conspicuous even at a distance—the rest of the tan body is dappled with light and dark green spots.) Junior was also persistent.

The ubiquitous blister vines whipped across my face and body as I fled through the forest, receiving a bloody gash above my eye and on my left breast. Their oily residue stung like hell, and the pain slowed me down. Think of semi-sentient and slightly mobile poison ivy on steroids, live whips that liked to pommel and grab.

Did I mention they sing? Little suckers along their lengths breathe in and out, making a high-pitched humming noise. (Unlike centaurs, poison ivy isn't mythical Earth flora, but it's long gone from planet Earth, thanks to the Tali invasion.) Their whipping action makes a bit of noise too.

The young drooler was just about to sink his teeth into me when I broke out into the clear and flew over the edge of the precipice, right across one of those lava rifts.

This one was narrow enough that I didn't fall in and become deep-fried Asako tempura, a fate I thought might still be better than being eaten by this carnivore. I hit a ledge four meters down on the opposite side so hard that I broke my leg and knocked the wind out. My pursuer, moving a bit slower, hit only the edge of the ledge, clawed desperately for a few seconds, and then crashed into the molten lava many meters below.

I felt sorry for him. He wouldn't be able to breed and pass his stupidity on to his offspring.

I then realized that the same could be said of me.

Chapter Two

Because Mom and Dad2 weren't studying Fistians, they didn't pay much attention to them. They knew Marcello and I were friends, but they didn't approve or disapprove. They were very focused on their work.

Mom studied the satellite's flora and fauna, so for her Fistians were like Humans—just one species among many surviving in a planetary ecosphere. She'd hinted one time that she admired the way the satellite's most intelligent lifeform took care of the environment, though. My perception was that their religion was pantheistic, if pantheism can be called a religion. As good an excuse as any for being environmentally conscious, I guess. They basically lived off the land, but I knew they hunted and fished sometimes.

Mom had participated in many studies during her career. One of the first was a visit to Earth to analyze how that planet was recovering from the Tali's attempts to destroy all of Earth's flora and fauna and replace it with that from their home world. Humans' last battles against the Tali occurred on Earth. The Tali lost, but now those remaining on our home planet were partners with Humans in restoring the original ecosphere as much as possible. Many species of animals and plants had become extinct, but there'd been some hidden arks where seeds and frozen fetuses were stored. The Humans who had built them were somewhat paranoid to my way of thinking, but now that paranoia was celebrated by everyone who lived on Earth, and by many Humans elsewhere in near-Earth space.

Mom was the most athletic member of my parental triad. She had no special physical characteristics—most Humans looked the same now, although a sharp eye could detect a few differences—but she wasn't a tall woman. Many Humans weren't tall because many of them had descended from the first colonists to leave Earth's solar system, and many of those were descended from Spacers in that home system, who tended to be small. Her short dark brown hair, expressive brown eyes, and tawny skin weren't unique by any means, but she was special to me. Her occasional but sweet hugs almost made up for not paying much attention to me and letting me run wild.

As often happens, Mom had met Dad1 and Dad2 on another scientific expedition.

***

Dad2 is an exogeologist, so his scientific field didn't overlap at all with Mom's. Because I have such a biased sample in our little scientific community, I don't know if that's common among Humans or not. It seems to me that romantic liaisons don't depend on what the members of a dyad or triad are doing in their professional lives, but I'm still collecting sociological data about that. Some say that it's better that dyad or triad members don't compete on a professional level. I could understand the reasons for saying that, but you never know.

Exogeology is an oxymoron all wrapped up in one word, of course—a word full of contradictions. "Geology" comes from "ge," meaning Earth. The word has its origin in some ancient Human language called Greek. The word came directly into Standard from English because the Mandarin words are also just a corruption of the ancient Greek. Adding "exo" is supposed to make it more general and apply everywhere.

Exogeology never interested me. Planets and their satellites only did when there were intelligent lifeforms on them with interesting cultures that I could study. I knew Fistian culture better than Human culture because of that. Hard Fist belonged to Fistians, not Humans. We were in the minority; I wanted to understand the majority. Maybe that was a provincial idea because of my friend Marcello and my first home being the same as his. But if you don't understand what you can directly experience, what can you understand?

Dad2 almost looked like he could be my Mom's brother. They weren't related at all, beyond being the modern version of Human, but, like I said, everyone looked very much the same now. He was more muscular than Mom, of course, but liked a more sedentary life as he studied the samples he gathered. He was quieter and less excitable than Mom too. As I lay on that ledge, I was thinking my parents and I had grown apart during the last few years. Easy to understand: I was older, so they thought I could take care of myself better.

It wasn't easy to discover any commonality between Fistians and Humans from interactions with my parents. That's often discounted by saying I wasn't an unbiased observer with respect to my parents, and I was more so with respect to Fistians. Maybe. I was close to them all, of course.

Yes, in spite of their preoccupation with work, I felt close to my parents, especially Dad2. While they were too aloof and engrossed with their research at times, and were often away on expeditions, I admired them. They knew a lot of cool stuff too. Because they'd had me later in their lives, and I was their only child, they probably spoiled me a little to compensate for not participating too much in my childhood. They were there when I needed them...usually.

Dad2 was literally digging into Hard Fist's past. He would hop into a rugged terrain vehicle or a water sled and disappear for weeks—not so long as Mom, but long. I'd gone on a few trips with him and soon became bored. When he returned from others, I would ask him about Fistians. He'd just shrug, said he'd seen some, and left it at that. He would then start telling me about strata and evidence for continental slippage, different rocks and ores, and so forth. It all seemed exciting to him, but not to me.

***

Compared to other monads, dyads, and triads in our scientific community, I thought I was lucky to have my parents. That's not saying much. I'd read a computer file once about kids called "military brats" back on Earth before any extensive exploration of the home solar system had occurred. They were kids who had to move around with their parents because one or both parents (I guess there were no triads back then) were in some military organization.

After reading that, I decided that I was a "science brat." I often dreaded the day when my parents would leave Hard Fist, and I would have to go with them. I wanted to hurry up and stop being a kid and become independent so that wouldn't happen. Now it seemed that there was no hurry. I was going to die right there on that ledge.

I had regrets about not getting to know my parents better. Also about dying, of course. I seemed too young to die. That led to some unusual introspection, a conversation with myself I'd never had.

Chapter Three

It's not easy to contemplate your premature death.

I was tempted to jump into the rift and let the lava consume me—at least I'd feel warm for a time—but I couldn't get to my feet with the pain in my leg. I probably could have tried rolling, but I wasn't sure whether there was another ledge beneath the one I was on. Rift walls aren't even. They're not even volcanic, just cracks in the terrain created by Big Fellow's squeezing and pulling rock and soil right down to the magma.

Just not my lucky day. Nearly baked by the sun during the 40 degree afternoon, I was now going to freeze in the minus 25 degree evening and night. Any warmth from that lava river seemed to blow right by me, but I suppose there was some benefit—I wouldn't freeze as fast as I would without it! On second thought, that would just prolong my misery.

Many other thoughts flew through my head, one of them being: *why did I try to follow that stupid Marcello? Maybe the other grown-ups and kids are right? Maybe they're just like prehistoric Humans, brutish and ugly Fistian Neanderthals not much good for anything?*

No, I didn't buy it. I knew Fistians too well. They had all the signs of one day developing a technical civilization. *If we allow that to happen!* We Humans have a mixed track record there. Probably others out in the galaxy had left us alone and let us grow and develop a technological society, yet we Humans often tend to act more out of convenience than lofty ideals. Too many times, we are like those first missionaries to Hawaii—snooty and vain know-it-alls, convinced that we are doing the right thing by mucking around with native cultures. I know my Earth history; a lot of it isn't pretty. In fact, with the almost apocalyptic era of the Chaos that occurred just before the Tali invasion, it was downright ugly on the home planet.

I then had my epiphany.

You always wonder what you're going to be when you grow up! Some of us think we know at an early age but still wonder if that will work out. Some change their plans several times on the way to adulthood. Others are more lost and just wonder what they're going to do. I'd sometimes thought about becoming an exobiologist like Mom or exogeologist like Dad2. They might even want that, although they never said anything about it, but I decided that it just wasn't what I wanted to do.

My epiphany at that moment? I decided I wanted to dedicate my life to studying native Fistians, Mother's People as they called themselves. I wanted to learn more about them—not from the biological point of view, and not about their home, but about their culture and history.

I knew Marcello was exceptional and much smarter than me. He would certainly help me. Through him, I had already learned a lot about his culture, but so little about his history that I thought there wasn't much to it. Although I already was the moon's leading Human expert on Fistians, mostly by default, I still wanted to know more—a lot more.

Once I decided this, I started to cry. That wasn't just being a stupid little girl in a desperate situation. It was finally deciding what you're going to do with your life and then realizing you aren't going to be able to do it. *Silly, stupid girl is right!* I was becoming emotional about everything.

That wasn't my normal state. I figured I was probably starting to feel the cold. *Maybe my feet are frostbitten?* I wiggled the toes of my good leg. They seemed OK. Couldn't feel the others, of course.

Pulled up my pants leg and saw bone. No wonder I couldn't jump into the lava river to end my life in a noble manner. Ice would win over fire; I had no choice in the matter. I would go into hypothermia and die before I froze—small comfort. Not much fresh blood on that awful break, though. I would survive if I didn't freeze to death.

I curled up into a ball still feeling sorry for myself and wished morning would soon come, but also hoping that if I were going to die, it would be the slow freeze and not from starvation. I looked up at Big Fellow. *Just get it over with!*

***

"Asako, are you down there?"

Am I dreaming or in shock? No, the voice had come from above. I looked up and saw the glowing yellow eyes of Marcello beaming down at me.

"How-how did you find me?"

"An uncle told me that you had followed me into the high country."

"Oh." I thought a moment. It's weird how the cold makes your thoughts sharper even as it's killing you. "How did he tell you that?"

"We'll worry about that later. Let me get you out of there. You look uncomfortable." *What an understatement!* "I'm going to look for some blister vines."

Oh, no! "I already know them personally. They're real scratchy, Marcello, and not very friendly."

"They're also strong. Unless you know where I can find some rope, they're our best bet."

17

He found a good strong vine and tossed the wriggling end down to me. Even though it was writhing around, madder than the drooler had been but fortunately without the drooler's weapons to do something about it beyond the sting, I managed to tie it around me. That made it angrier because my torso was covering some of its breathing holes.

"Ready?" said Marcello.

I tightened the blister vine more. "As much as I'll ever be." I hopped on one foot to the edge of the chasm. *Good thing I didn't think of that before! Here goes!* I jumped into the rift.

Marcello held tight as I crashed into the steep wall on his side of the rift. The air whooshed out of my lungs again, but I held on and recovered as he hauled me up.

"Can you get on my back?"

"I think so." It was a struggle, but I fought through the pain, grabbed some mane, and off he galloped.

***

On that ride I reflected on what a good friend Marcello was. I had only become seriously mad at him one time. We'd journeyed into the hills to that same high country above his village and stopped at a natural overlook.

"I sat here one night and looked at the stars," he'd said, waving both of his expressive hands as if he were unveiling the heavens.

He was sitting on his rump, as usual, and I sat in a lotus position. I looked out over the rainforests of Hard Fist to the ocean's shore and beyond. I'd been on those beaches, both alone and with Marcello. How could he compare that view to little points of light in a sky that were usually blurred by humidity?

"I'd rather be here in the daytime," I said. "You can't have this wonderful view of Hard Fist at night. And I wouldn't have to bundle up so much against the cold."

"But Hard Fist is only one place among many. Our Universe is huge, with many stars and planets and satellites. Think of all the wonderful adventures awaiting us out there!"

Is Marcello becoming a scientist, or does he just have some explorer genes?

"I suppose there are some interesting cultures out there," I said, "but you must be on a planet or a satellite to study them. Understanding different cultures seems like a nobler pursuit. Without people wondering about the Universe, it just becomes a cold, foreboding place."

"We'll have to agree to disagree about that. I could be all alone in the Universe and still get turned on by studying its natural phenomena—stars, planets, black holes, novae, colliding stars—there are many things to understand. The other villagers think more like you do, though, all selfishly wrapped up in their own lives."

"Selfishly? Fistians are very outgoing! From what I've seen, they're a lot more gregarious than my own people, including Mom and Dad2."

"Your parents are studying Hard Fist, not what's beyond Hard Fist. Their focus is wrong. In a thousand years, nobody will care about what they discover here, but the Universe will still go on. It has a permanence. So does everything we learn about it."

"So the different cultures don't count for anything?"

"Not for me."

We sat in silence after that, and I also rode him back to the village in silence. I don't know which is worse: the mental anguish of a disagreement, or the physical anguish of a broken body.

We had been very young, but it was an interesting lesson: You can be close friends with someone even if you don't agree on everything.

***

I'd been a bit churlish with Marcello because he had made me angry, but I wasn't immune to the wonders of our universe, more about the aesthetics than about scientific details. Not too many places would have Big Fellow hanging in the sky, for example. Even in the daytime, it was a pale jewel floating there in all its splendor.

Big Fellow and the Fistian sun are almost a double star system because the gas giant is nearly massive enough to be a star. The local sun is a bit weaker than Earth's, but Big Fellow is a bit closer to it. The Fistian year is shorter than a standard year as a consequence.

There are seasons on Hard Fist, but not the kind you would see on Earth or some other planets. Big Fellow's axis was tilted, but Hard Fist's orbital plane was too, and in the opposite direction. The two tilts didn't exactly cancel, though, so Hard Fist's climate changes were less than those of Big Fellow, if a gas giant can be said to have seasons. Like on Jupiter and Saturn, this gas giant had cyclone storms that sometimes lasted for hundreds of years.

I found it strange that there weren't scientists on Hard Fist studying Big Fellow. RF radiation from it often played havoc with our com systems, for example. Or someone could study those impressive storms that I guessed might be the cause of the RF interference. Dad2 said this scientific neglect was probably because all gas giants are similar, and Human scientists had learned a lot about the ones in the home system before the Tali invasion. That info had arrived at the original colonies as part of the databases on those old colony ships.

I wondered if Marcello would take up the study of Big Fellow. He was curious, and he'd be able to do it while staying home. An adventurous yen to see as much of the universe as he could might nix that idea, though. I certainly wasn't going to push him one way or the other.

***

Marcello might be more fascinated by the so-called hard sciences, more so as time went on, but I saw them as a means to an end: I needed to know something about them to get through school, but I knew I also needed them to live in a technological society. That was about it for me.

That had led to some confrontations in our school. Because our group of scientists was small, and they shared teaching duties without having much preparation to teach, you can guess how those confrontations might occur. Write it off as my rebellion against an over-emphasis on hard science.

I was also the oldest student. All the kids were all thrown together. Each kid went at his own pace. Because patience isn't one of my virtues, I tended to fly through the lessons and make mistakes. My problem with school: The personal attention was OK; the emphasis wasn't. I was bored by the subjects they emphasized.

Mom and Dad2 were the hardest on me. They wanted me to excel in everything. What I wanted to excel in, even before my epiphany, was barely covered.

The major confrontation with Mom was over evolution.

"Evolution is a force of nature," I'd written in one report probably still buried in its computer file. "It has nothing to do with forces of nature as we know them from physics," Mom had indicated in red, bold font. "It comes from a competition between species. Over millions of years, species compete. Some win, some lose." "Intelligent life begins when one species becomes dominant," I wrote. "There are plenty of biospheres where that doesn't happen," Mom wrote, "and sometimes two or more intelligent lifeforms arise." She also wrote at the bottom of the last page of the computer file, "Opinions don't count in science. Back up your opinions with facts. You have access to a powerful AI." I received a 5 out of 10 on that report.

"Rocks and strata are formed from upheavals in a non-stellar object," I'd written in a exogeology report. "Satellites can also be artificial," Dad2 wrote in a red font, but eschewing bold, "and you need to give examples. Lava creates basalt, for example. Some materials are morphed into others by compression." "Satellites are affected by their proximity to the planet they orbit," I wrote. "See comment above," Dad2 wrote. I thought that was unfair because even an artificial satellite's orbit is affected by the planet it orbits. I told Dad2 he was nitpicking, but I couldn't complain much because he'd given me an 8 out of 10 on that report.

I cared more about the grades from my parents, of course, and not so much about the others.

***

Time passed. I began to make my epiphany that had come to me on that ledge become reality, not just wishful thinking. Much to my parents' surprise, I became a top student, received a scholarship from all the Human scientists on Hard Fist, and left at fifteen to study exosociology on the planet Sanctuary in the δ Pavonis system.

PART II:
SANCTUARY

A.B. CAROLAN

Chapter Four

My trip to Sanctuary was safe and uneventful. That's a nice way to say boring. The crewmembers of the Space Exploration Bureau's starship weren't used to having fifteen-year-olds around and ignored me as much as the scientists on Hard Fist did because most of them were busy recording what was learned on the missions to planets they'd visited before arriving at Hard Fist. I killed time looking at random computer files and playing games with the ship's AI.

Part of the problem was that there were no other young people on board. Many SEB ships have young interns in the crews, but the youngest crewmember on this one was the captain who was a few centuries my senior. I felt lucky that I could hitch a ride, of course, but I would have liked something more to do.

In hindsight, I guess I learned a bit how starships function, even a small one, and decided I didn't enjoy being on one. Once that decision was made I could get a head start on my studies. In the computer library there were even copies of competency exams in various subjects. I wanted to pass as many of those as I could in order to finish my basic degree in record time.

Sanctuary is one of the original three Human colonies. I suppose colonists in that old pioneering starship were just too tired to go elsewhere after such a long trip—over one hundred years back then with most adult travelers in cryosleep accompanied in their slumbers by thousands of frozen embryos, ova, and sperm in order to contribute genetic diversity to the new colony. But the planet still wasn't a very nice reward for traveling all that distance and all those years because it was so inhospitable. The entire population had to live in domes from day one, and they still lived in them, although there were now many more now scattered across the planet's surface because of the increase in the number of inhabitants.

From space, that rocky and desolate place looks like it's covered with clusters of the ground nests of that large insect-like Fistian creature. You can see rocket exhaust from an occasional flitter traveling from one cluster to another. More activity could be seen around the spaceports. The planet is now a major hub for near-Earth trade. δ Pavonis is a G8 star and only twenty light-years from Earth, and many other planets snatch up what Sanctuary manufactures.

The planet is famous for the desperate battle fought against Tali invaders, Humans managing to defeat them in spite of being outnumbered and with fewer and more primitive weapons. Their Guide to the Way, Brent Mueller, organized everyone into a determined defense force the likes of which Tali had never encountered before in their conquests. Colonists from the first Human colonies had eventually helped to defeat the Tali on Earth too.

I knew some of Sanctuary's history but was unprepared for life in the domes. They weren't defensive at all. Instead, they were engineered to contain artificial environments for Humans because the atmosphere outside was still toxic, although terraforming operations had been cleaning it up over the centuries. They had developed hydroponics engineering into a fine art within the domes. And many specialized industries as well.

But I was there to study the techniques used to catalog and understand sociological organizations, particularly those among non-Humans. There weren't many of the latter on Sanctuary in general, but I soon met some at the university.

***

I stayed with some old friends of my parents. They had three children, all younger than me—I shared a room with the oldest girl—so I'd flee to the huge university library when they became too rowdy. We still had a good time, though, when I wasn't busy with my studies. It was fun to stay in touch with my childhood, but I think I was generally too serious for them. My goal was to make great academic leaps forward and return as soon as possible to Hard Fist to do the research required for my thesis.

The library wasn't my only hangout. I also found refuge in something called a bookstore. That was something new for me, but it was like a library in the sense that I could rent computer files by the hour and read them, or I could rent them for a longer period and transfer them to my university account. I was into everything. Einstein, our AI on Hard Fist, had many limitations. Even the AI on the starship that brought me to Sanctuary was more advanced.

The bookstore was run by a Human and Tali. The Tali was a pleasant fellow—from talking to him you couldn't imagine their bellicose past and hatred for all lifeforms not from a Tali world redone to their specifications. People change—for the better, in this case. I met the Human the third time I was there. His name was Carolan. I asked him what kind of name that was.

"Why, Human of course." He smiled. "But to elaborate, I delve into genealogy, not an easy matter, considering the Tali invasion of Earth. My ancestor was in the first colony ship to Novo Mondo. We can trace our line all the way back to some place called Ireland. As near as I can tell, it's some country that existed on Earth before the Chaos."

I nodded. The Tali invasion wasn't the only thing that had destroyed old Earth records. Ireland was probably a country that existed before the Chaos, a wild era in Earth's history, had created havoc in Earth's social structures and eventually led to the colony ships. In retrospect, that was a good thing, because without the Earth colonies, Humans probably would no longer be around.

"I don't suppose there are many records left from that time," I said.

"If you find some, please tell me. I'm always interested. Not just in genealogy, but in general history. We're expanding so fast in near-Earth space that we lose sight of our history. That's sad."

The library and bookstore were more than distractions. They allowed me to skip a lot of general courses by passing that battery of competency exams. After a brief vacation back on Hard Fist to catch my breath, I returned once again to Sanctuary for degree work.

My life turned from academic drudgery to academic paradise when I met Lonely Swimmer.

***

Lonely Swimmer is a Ranger from New Haven, that planet in the 82 Eridani system where Humans had their first encounter with another intelligent lifeform. I had to admire how open-minded those New Haven Human colonists must have been because Rangers are the strangest ETs Humans have ever encountered, much stranger than Fistians. Yet they'd become our willing collaborators in making our little corner of the galaxy safe by helping Humans create ITUIP, the Interstellar Trade Union of Independent Planets. And two physicists, one Human and the other Ranger, had created the theory for the FTL drive that made all that possible.

I pushed the door buzzer and heard a computer's voice in my head say, "Come in. I've been expecting you." I'd been fitted with one of those wi-fi implants in the side of my head when I'd returned to Sanctuary and was still getting used to it. It allowed me to access computer files from almost anywhere. More importantly, it allowed me to understand my new thesis adviser.

The door slid open. I stepped into an artificial cavern filled with a dull blue light. The walls were finished to look like rock, and the floor was fine sand. The humidity reminded me of Hard Fist, but the air was cold—not as cold as a Fistian night, of course, but colder than I liked. It didn't seem to bother Lonely Swimmer, but I knew winters on New Haven could be rough, so maybe he was immune to the cold.

"Come join me in the tank," said the computer's voice. I touched the wi-fi implant attached behind my right ear. The direct communication was so different from what I was used to on Hard Fist. Marcello and I hadn't needed it because my friend spoke Standard. "There's a ladder."

What I'd taken as a curved wall in front of me was the edge of a tank, the entire tank only slightly bigger than a Fistian home. A ladder scaled it.

"Is it water?" I said, remembering the Rangers were water-loving, but I didn't want to make dangerous assumptions.

"Of course. I have certain extra privileges as Department Chairperson, but this tank is essential for my

29

survival. Your records state you know how to swim, among other things."

Thought about the cold. Didn't want to turn blue in ice cold water. There was plenty of opportunity to swim on Hard Fist. The water was warm—generally around eighteen degrees for the oceans. I loved body surfing, in fact, and snorkeling along the reefs. They weren't coral on Hard Fist—they had gone extinct on Earth—but lava walls left by ancient flows from Big Fellow's kneading of its satellite.

I climbed the ladder high enough to look over the tank's edge. The tank was toroidal, and the water was swirling around the ring, making it appear more like a slow river than a lake or pond. Rivers on Hard Fist were wider and swifter. Probably warmer too. I didn't know about New Haven's.

A head bobbed up beneath me. A tentacle from around the Ranger's mouth snaked toward me, the hand-end patting me on my forehead with a redolent, wet, and cold touch, but everything about Sanctuary seemed cold. The people there saved on power by keeping ambient temperatures in the domes much lower than even those of our air conditioned dwellings on Hard Fist. I'd started to wear a thick pullover soon after I arrived.

"Are you Professor Lonely Swimmer?" I said.

"At your service, Human child."

"And you want me to join you?"

"I can get to know you better by scanning you with ultrasound pulses underwater. Indulge me but for a moment. I don't imagine you have a change of clothes, so remove what you have on and join me. We'll do a few laps too. I understand it's great exercise for Humans as well as a basic necessity for Rangers."

I removed my clothes and jumped in, surviving the cold and the strange experience of being quizzed by my new thesis adviser in that fashion, We both let the artificial current carry us around the torus. I could slow down by swimming against it and speed up by swimming with it. Either option let me shake off some of the cold with body heat generated from exertion. I didn't think much of that first experience, but I soon adapted to her desire to swim every day. The water always seemed too cold, though.

I didn't expect a Ranger to be too comfortable out of water, but she was. She was almost as nimble and quick on land as in the water. Our discussions often took place in her office where she'd jump onto the high chair behind her desk so our eyes were at the same level. They were located just above and on each side of her mouth that was surrounded by tentacles, two of which ended in those soft and sensitive hands. She looked a bit like a drawing I'd seen of a termite, but she was covered by soft fur. Their homes on New Haven were generally found in caverns by ponds, lakes, and rivers that iced up in winter.

One person isn't representative of an entire group, of course, but I liked Lonely Swimmer, and she taught me a lot. I taught her some things too because she didn't know anything about Fistians and was anxious to learn. We became much more than professor and student. We became friends.

Chapter Five

In my third week after my return to Sanctuary, I met Bobby. Roberto Schmidt approached my table at the library one day. I studied this boy with his blond curls, penetrating blue eyes, and ready smile. He looked familiar.

"You're back," he said. He pulled out a chair and sat opposite me.

He seemed to be my age and just a bit taller; an attractive fellow, he was slender and muscular. He was the first student who had paid much attention to me. He possessed a casual but confident air about him that seemed to say I should be impressed, and I was, but I naturally wondered.

"Excuse me? Do I know you?"

"An admirer from afar," he said with a smile, "from your first time here." He offered a fist for a fist-bump. "Bobby Schmidt. We started some courses together, but you opted out of those requirements by passing competency tests. Are you an android?"

An insult? Human culture can vary from planet to planet. I'd experienced the fist-bump on Sanctuary. It seemed to be the universal greeting on the planet, but I'd heard the handshake was used more on the worlds of near-Earth space. "Meaning?"

"I could never be that focused and study all that stuff in such a short time. I'd have to become an android plugged into an AI all the time." He began to spin his notepad computer around. *He's nervous.* "We'll live a long time, you know. Why not have some fun?"

"I happen to have a busy agenda and little time for fun. I already miss my home planet, but there are things I have to attend to here. Did you finish the study program?"

"Way behind you. I'm taking my time. I plan to take next year off, in fact, to do a bit of exploring off-planet."

I think I understand his motivation, but who's paying?

"Not much to explore here," I said, although I didn't know enough about Sanctuary to backup that statement.

"Off-planet's probably more interesting, but there are some interesting places here too. You haven't seen all of Sanctuary, I bet."

I shook my head. *Guilty as charged.* I offered an excuse. "Please don't take offense, but it's a claustrophobic, dreary place."

He shrugged. "I'm used to it, so it doesn't make me claustrophobic. It's dark and dreary, I'll admit. But I can show you some fun spots."

"Why me? I've seen you talking to lots of girls." I'd just remembered why he looked familiar.

"So you've been admiring me too?"

"Just because you seem so friendly and carefree." *A bit of a lie.* It was because he was good-looking. "I guess that goes along with taking your time about finishing the program."

"Let me say you shine like a supernova compared to all those other girls. You're an exotic creature. They're all so dull and boring."

Exotic? I'd never been called exotic. I wore my hair short and didn't use a lot of makeup like Sanctuary girls. I was already taller than Mom and almost as tall as Dad2, but Dad1 had been taller, so I didn't have any way to determine if I was through growing—generally speaking, the Human female doesn't grow much beyond thirteen, so I was probably on the edge.

Dad2 always said I had an impish look—the girl with twinkling, mischievous eyes, he'd say. I took that as a compliment and a complement to my generally positive outlook on life. Right then, I suspect my eyes expressed surprise and annoyance.

I also dressed comfortably—in other words, simply. Again, not like Sanctuary girls, who tended to dress skimpily in revealing clothes—I couldn't because the domes were too cold for me. I'd never been one to covet worldly goods either, valuing data, scientific records, and analyses over jewelry and expensive toys even before I learned to walk—or so my parents said.

My appearance matched my outlook—simple and practical…and focused on things most girls my age weren't focused on. I could appear to be an exotic off-world creature to the local youths.

"I guess I'll take that as a compliment. But now you can go away. I have work to do."

He nodded. "Sure thing, if you promise to let me show you around Sanctuary to see the sights sometime."

We made a date. I did it more to make him go away, but even at the time I suspected that caving in wasn't a good idea.

***

As a local resident, Bobby knew Sanctuary and its history better than I did, of course. In spite of limited real estate within the domes, there was much to see and understand both inside and outside. He made the Battle of Sanctuary come to life by taking me to places where some of the action had occurred in that fight for survival against the Tali. Learning that even children had fought and perished in that battle was humbling. My goals for my work on Hard Fist seemed trivial in comparison, but I lived in different times.

He told me how Brent Mueller, the main Guide to the Way at the time the Talis attacked, planned the defense of the domes, only to lose the mayor, a strong, intelligent woman he loved, in the battle. That loss had turned him from the Way, that strange philosophy that became popular in Earth's solar system back in the years of the Chaos. I thought the story of that battle should be better known—it was the stuff of legends. I was also embarrassed to learn that Mueller had played an important role in near-Earth history on other occasions. He had lived a long time.

For example, Bobby also took me to the Dark Domes where Brent Mueller and others fought to save an SEB scientist named Silvia Kensington from a brutal industrialist (my parents also worked for the Space Exploration Bureau, an ITUIP agency). I'd never heard that history before, and it involved Swarm.

I decided that Swarm made Fistians and Rangers and all other ET cultures in near-Earth space seem boringly normal. That strange collective intelligence of millions of minds in a star cluster went crazy at times, but it was instrumental in stopping both the Tali and the sociopathic industrialist.

"How did you learn all these historical details?" I said as we walked in the silence of the Dark Domes neighborhood.

"My mother is a historian," Bobby said. "She knows a bit about ET cultures but only in regards to their interactions with Humans. She's always trying to prove that without Humans, ITUIP would never have come into being and become a success."

"That sounds like a bit of a stretch. Rangers, Tali, and others had their own cultures when Humans were still living in caves. Or even before. Fistians too."

He shrugged. "And the Chinese had gone through several dynasties by the time Europe began settling North and South America. That didn't stop the West from ignoring the East until after the Chinese colonized Mars." He smiled. "And could the Chinese have done that without the advances made in the U.S. and U.S.S.R. space programs? Probably not. History is full of events where groups chose the wrong road to travel down." I thought that was somewhat perceptive, but he was probably just repeating his mother's opinions. "Are you tired?"

I was leaning against a huge tank. "A bit. And cold. Maybe we should get back. I need to go to the library. I'm a bit behind in my work."

He pinned me against the tank and tried to kiss me. I turned my face away.

"I have feelings for you, Asako."

Those feelings were evident in the bulge of his pants. "I'm not ready for that commitment, Bobby."

"You don't like me?"

"Maybe. I don't know. Just don't rush me."

He backed off and shrugged again. "OK. You don't know what you're missing."

Yeah, I did. I ached for him. But something restrained me.

Chapter Six

Bobby and I continued to see each other, and I even let him kiss me a few times. It was a struggle to keep it at that. I was getting tired of his advances, though, so I hesitated when he invited me to dinner at his place.

"Relax," he said. "We won't be alone. My parents want to meet you. They're always butting in, but their intentions are good, I guess. It will be fun. My father's a scientist too."

"What kind?"

"Maybe not a scientist. An applied mathematician. He works on improving AI technology for starships. They're so complicated now that Humans can't really react fast enough even in ordinary space. 'Course they never could even before when crossing through metaverses after going FTL."

I'd read and listened to all sorts of explanations about how faster-than-light drives tapped into zero-point fields for enough energy to negotiate the strange topologies of multiple universes. It was all a swindle in the sense that going from point A to B in our Universe was accomplished essentially by avoiding the space-time between A and B.

We learned long ago that the best theory for explaining our observed universe implies the existence of others. Moreover, mathematical formulations involved in superstring theory describe a vast number of quantum vacuum states. Those many states can be interpreted as descriptions of multiple universes. Once physicists got past fanciful dark matter conjectures to explain galactic dynamics and realized that it and dark energy was an expression of their ignorance, things started to fall into place and creative invention took over.

And that's about all I know. I'm not even sure I got that right. But I expected Bobby's father to lose me in seconds if he ever talked about his work, especially if he only talked mathematics. I could handle some advanced mathematics—I'd learned some group theory and differential equations long ago—but expert mathematicians might as well write in the runes of an ancient stellar civilization and speak their language as far as I was concerned.

"Sounds complicated."

"I guess so. The SEB pays him a lot of money. Makes a lot more than Mom."

"Different work," I said. "That pay difference is only wrong if they're doing the same work. That still happens on many planets, but most ITUIP planets are fair."

Bobby had his own cart—his family was well off. The vehicle, a three-wheeled one with hard rubber tires that could scoot silently around domes and through their connecting tunnels, was completely electric. We parked it in its assigned space and entered his parents' apartment complex. Their apartment was ten floors down.

Dinner was cordial, even pleasant, until we began discussing my thesis.

"Why do you want to study Fistians?" Bobby's mother said. She was a large, frumpy woman with a long nose. I guessed Bobby's parents hadn't believed in genetic engineering—or rather the grandparents hadn't. Bobby seemed a perfect physical specimen. "Seems like a waste of time."

"They're my friends, and Humans don't know enough about them."

"I wish it could stay that way," said the father. He had heavy jowls and blinked a lot. "Even here in Sanctuary you see ETs all over the place. It irks me that our taxes pay for special dwellings and habitats for some of them."

I thought of Lonely Swimmer's tank. "Let's suppose Bobby develops an incurable nerve disease that leaves him paraplegic. Wouldn't you want to build things to help him get around? Buy him an electric wheelchair maybe? Special prosthetics? Expect research to be done on how to cure him?"

"Not the same thing," said his mother. "Those are medical necessities. Besides, that would never happen. My son's genetically perfect."

I stopped myself from saying something harsh. After all, I was their guest.

"Accidents can happen where the results aren't reversible. And if an ET lives and works on Sanctuary making valuable contributions to ITUIP's general society or culture, what then? Seems to me that providing him with special facilities benefits everyone in all the near-Earth planets."

I was becoming annoyed and wanted this conversation to stop, but I also wasn't going to let them run me over verbally.

"That hypothetical ET would just be taking a job away from a Human," said the father. "Not to mention using services like air and water Humans need in the domes. QED, my dear. Who's your suffering thesis adviser?"

I pushed away from the table. "Lonely Swimmer, chairperson of the Exosociology Department at the university." I walked out.

"That settles that," I heard Bobby's mother say. "Stay away from that girl, Bobby. She's a no good trouble-maker, and her thesis adviser is a water-bug."

Was pretty sure Bobby's parents would also call Marcello a centaur. It felt good to flee that home filled with bigotry. I'd wasted enough energy trying to argue with them.

***

Bobby still tried to talk to me several times on campus after that. He even tried to apologize for his parents. I saw some of them in him, though, so I ended the relationship. I saw no future in trying to reform his parents either. The best I could hope for was that their son wouldn't become too much like them. Bobby and I went from being close friends to casual acquaintances.

I couldn't call him my first love, but he might have become that. Decided it was better to know how he and his family thought before we'd become serious. *Am I a centaur- and water-bug-lover?* The question didn't even make sense to me. You have to reserve judgement about everyone, don't you? And judge them for what they say and do, not by how they look? But I did like a lot more Fistians than Humans, and Lonely Swimmer was now a good friend too.

I felt no regrets and soon looked at the positive: I'd seen and learned a lot about Sanctuary.

That year on Sanctuary was a prep year to defend my thesis proposal. Lonely Swimmer was a relentless taskmaster, and I thanked her for it. Step one: do the prep. Step two: write the proposal. Step three: defend it. Sounds simple. I knew other students took years to march through that gauntlet. I didn't want to take years. I was itching to continue my research.

The university's AI was a big help. Like Hard Fist's Einstein, Galileo often overloaded me with information dumps that I would have to sift through, only he did it more thoroughly. The bookstore owners were a great help too, especially with more obscure information. I soon developed search techniques to help find even more relevant information, and algorithms to help sift through all the data.

The process made me realize the importance of my planned research. Hard Fist was a satellite ITUIP's SEB had discovered and written off as not appropriate for colonization by any people from its member planets. First strike: the harsh climate. Second strike: the gravitational influence of Big Fellow; from landslides, earthquakes, and tsunamis, to those lava rivers, the satellite was considered hazardous. Third strike: there was already a large population of ETs on the planet. No one knew how many, but SEB estimated them to be more numerous than Rangers were on New Haven when Humans encountered them there. New Haven at that time would also have been declared unsuitable for colonization, but those first Human colonists didn't have much choice—they didn't know Rangers were there, and they'd spent over a century getting there.

Three strikes? I didn't know why SEB considered three significant. I would have added droolers and blister vines as strikes against Hard Fist, but maybe SEB didn't care about them. I would have to start my thesis with all that information from ITUIP and counter it with the fact that I and other Humans called Hard Fist home. I also thought Sanctuary in its original state was a terrible candidate for colonization, and now it was still a terrible place to live—that also negated ITUIP's position a bit in my mind.

And none of the strikes mattered if Hard Fist later petitioned to become a member of ITUIP, right?

Chapter Seven

"Your body is designed for water," I said to Lonely Swimmer. "You have an unfair advantage. Mine isn't." I was sitting on a rung of the ladder that led into the tank. That was really an excuse. The water seemed colder that day. Sitting wet in the cold air didn't help my mood either.

She laughed at me. "For both land and water. When the Human body doesn't adapt to an environment, you adapt the environment to the body. We could get you some floaters and fins, for example. But you're learning to swim better, Asako. Your body can move fast in the water despite your Human limitations. Did you know Annie Li was a good swimmer? *Au naturel,* too, without any assistance from devices."

That sounded like an old Earth language. Or was the computer having fun at my expense? It probably knew all the old languages! "The theoretical physicist?" I thought a moment. "Even before she met Deep Breather?"

Long ago on New Haven, the brilliant duo of the Human Annie Li and the Ranger Deep Breather created the theory that led to the faster-than-light star drive. I didn't understand the complicated theory, as I indicated before, but knew that sociologically the invention of FTL changed the course of history in near-Earth space for all intelligent lifeforms, and it made the ITUIP possible.

"I'm not sure about that. They certainly swam together after they met. Just like you and me." Lonely Swimmer emphasized her point by pointing to me and her with one delicate hand on the end of a mouth-tentacle.

I felt honored that she compared us to that famous pair but decided modesty was in order. "But you're my mentor. They were equals."

"For our understanding of Fistian culture, you are my mentor. A professor who doesn't learn from her students doesn't deserve to be a professor."

Embarrassed by that, I decided to change the topic. "Do you miss New Haven?"

"That's a complicated question but probably worthy of an answer. Let me tell you how I came to be here, little Human."

***

"Three of us were being groomed to be clan mother for a new clan that we needed to create." I thought of Mama Dora. Matriarchal societies were common. "A Human in that original New Haven colony had discovered a mutation among our people that had reduced our birthrates; she taught us how to solve the problem, so our population was growing. We seemed to be making up for lost time."

"While I knew it was a considerable honor to be so chosen, I didn't want to be a clan mother. They must be great storytellers and keep the lengthy history of our people and their clan in their memories. We had no written history; even now we depend a lot on Human computer technology. Back then our brains were always loaded with other memories." As she treaded water, she clasped the two hands at the end of her principal tentacles together. "We have two languages, as you know. One you Humans call buzzspeak—the one the AI translates to Standard and back. The other is our water language, where we transmit sonar pictures describing our aquatic surroundings as we swim. Or probe them, as I did with you when we first met. That's plenty for most

Rangers to keep straight with little room to spare except when you have a genius like our mathematical physicist Deep Breather."

"And I was interested in other knowledge, not our history. I wanted to study social organizations in other ET cultures. I felt we didn't understand them well enough. Ian Holst's father began the studies of Ranger culture on New Haven and deserves as much fame as his son, the engineer who turned the FTL theory into practical interstellar travel. I wanted to do the father's kind of research. Many that was impractical, but it's what I wanted to do."

I could sympathize with that viewpoint. It was my own in regards to Fistians. She did another lap around the tank before continuing.

"I spent many years on the Tali home world; I also spent time on the Usk home world. That led to three academic works that established me as an exosociologist: one each for the Tali and Usks, and the third a comparative study of the two analyzing their similarities and differences. I then came to Sanctuary because I conjectured that domes here could produce a social structure something akin to our clans. A clan's pond defines the clan; a Human's dome on this planet defines the residents in that dome. That situation seemed to merit another study, and so I did it."

"Of course, now that similarity is disappearing as the planetary populations of Rangers on New Haven and Humans on Sanctuary increase in numbers and become planetary societies rather than independent groups, and even beyond within the Interstellar Trade Union of Independent Planets. But that process is interesting and worthy of study too."

***

Lonely Swimmer seemed lost in thought for a moment, but then she continued.

"I was reluctant to become head of this department, though. Your Human bureaucracy cuts down on my research time and the time I can spend with students. I haven't had that many students, in fact, and I rather enjoy those experiences. Young minds are more creative and open to new ideas. They want to expand the frontiers of knowledge. By working with them, we old ones can stay young."

"The politics disturb me more than mere bureaucracy, though. Because we're so different from most intelligent lifeforms, we have to deal with xenophobia too, just like your Fistians. I tend to experience it more because Rangers rarely come to Sanctuary to live. It's not exactly a water world." I smiled at that joke. "We're a small minority even compared to the Tali. The numbers of those who despise us aren't many, but their hatred for us is often all too obvious."

"That didn't happen on New Haven when Humans and Rangers first met."

"A fortuitous circumstance. Or maybe because we were the first to arrive there."

"And you soon had a common enemy."

"That's perceptive of you. The Tali destroyed our home world as they did yours. I have on my bucket list—I believe that's what Humans call it, although I don't know why—a trip to both my home world and Earth to see how they've recovered."

"I've never been to either one. That would be an interesting trip to make."

"All in good time, Asako."

Chapter Eight

When you're busy, time flies, but I took some more time off to have some fun. Bobby had given me a yen to explore Sanctuary a bit more and meet a few more people. Although it would surprise Dad2, I even joined a club of exogeology students who went out exploring on the surface dressed in masks and suits, looking to improve their ground-penetrating radar. The local exogeologists used it to detect heavy metallic ores close to Sanctuary's surface. I suppose Dad2 and his colleagues knew all about that, but I wanted to mention it to Lars Swensen. Could he use it to find artifacts and skeletons?

Denise Amalfi was in the group, and we became good friends. Dad2 and Denise are as different as night and day, though. She had already defended her thesis project.

"It's not so bad," she said to me one day when we were having lunch together in one of the university's dining halls. "You must get your thesis committee involved early so the defense just becomes a formality. If they want you to succeed, you will."

She was a bit older than me but less focused. She was a brown giant with wonderfully kinky hair who was born on a planet that had just been admitted to ITUIP. Both her parents had come from Earth, of all places, by way of Novo Mondo, another one of the three original Human colonies.

She put away food as if famine were imminent. I watched her polish off something called a sub. Sub what, I don't know—it was filled with all kinds of stuff. She said it was an Earth invention. I hadn't experienced much of anything from Earth. First, a lot of things hadn't survived the Tali invasion and were only mentioned in computer files on the starships that had arrived at those original three Human colonies. Second, I was from Hard Fist. The Human diet was plain and utilitarian there, and the Fistian diet was even more so and based on local products.

I watched her pack away her lunch while I picked at something bland called a tofu salad. That I understood. Almost all food on the starships I'd flown on was based on soy. They might call it something like roast beef, but it was just some form of soy. I guessed the stuff was easy to grow, and the starship could store great quantities of it at every port.

"What happens if some committee member objects to what I'm doing?"

"Make sure that they all want you to succeed, that's all." She stretched and yawned. Because she was older, her breasts were fully developed. I envied her. I smiled at that thought, though. *Without Bobby in the picture, what do I care?* "I admire you, Asako."

That twist surprised me. "Why? You're well on your way to your doctorate. I'm only beginning."

"But you really stay focused. For me, there are a lot of distractions."

"Boys?"

She smiled. "No, my music. I have a group. We modeled ourselves after some of those 21st century girl-bands. I'm principal on drums and alternate bass guitar. Part of the backup chorus too."

"Sounds more like a hobby," I said.

"We've been offered a touring contract. The others want to do it. I'm still not committed."

"Keep mulling it over. When you decide what you want to do, you'll get focused."

"What do you recommend?"

"I've never heard your group. Invite me to a concert."

She did just that, only she called it a gig. I soon realized Denise had a hard choice to make. The band was good. My only real Human friend on Sanctuary hadn't made up her mind before I left. Part of the problem was that two girls in the band wanted to form a triad with her, and she was enjoying their attention...so girls, not boys, *were* involved in her lack of focus on her thesis. Yet she knew that the entertainment industry only rarely offered a secure job; exogeology was a safer profession in that sense.

I went to a few more gigs, but the thesis project defense loomed.

***

"You'll have to do a lot of work breaking down barriers," said Mekan, a Tali who was on my thesis committee.

We were celebrating the successful defense of my thesis project in a fancy restaurant near the university. Lonely Swimmer, Mekan, and four Humans made up my committee. The general consensus was that I was smart enough to do what I wanted to do as my research, but could I leap over all the cultural hurdles that awaited me back on Hard Fist? In the defense of my thesis project, I had spent a lot of time arguing that I could. I had also overcome many committee members' perceptions that I was too young. Mekan thought those two problems were linked. He was the most doubtful.

"Working with primitive societies is always a challenge," said Gil Mosely, one of the Human committee members. He took a sip of havenberry brandy Sanctuary imported from New Haven. I drank non-alcoholic havenberry juice as a bow to Sanctuary norms about underage drinking. Marcello would have laughed at that, knowing how much I liked fermented Fistian drinks. "Take it slow."

"Fistians aren't primitive," I said. "They're just different."

"Guess you'll have to prove that," said Mekan.

"Asako will accept that as a challenge," said Lonely Swimmer, Galileo translating her buzzspeak into perfect Standard. She was sitting on a high chair designed for Rangers. "Please remember, my dear, we're only interested in facts. Whatever you find out about them will be more than we know now. That's what motivates everyone here, the discovery of new knowledge. Who knows what surprises you might find?" She picked up a fish with those delicate fingers on the end of her tentacle, tossed it inside her mouth, and then washed it down with the same brandy, which they'd invented, of course. "But I'll go beyond Dr. Mosely's warning. Do be careful. Don't become overconfident just because you were born on Hard Fist. You've lived a sheltered life there, and also from the rest of the galaxy. Keep an open mind."

"How long do I have?" It was a logical question now that the thesis project was approved.

"As long as you need," said Mekan. "We'll still be here to listen to your brilliant thesis defense whenever you're finished. And I do expect it to be brilliant."

Great! What do they call that? Being a victim of my own success? Everyone at the table thought I was a genius but me. I was just an innocent, bewildered, and frail girl trying to understand Marcello and his people, the best friends I'd ever had.

***

I told Denise about the defense of my thesis plan. She shrugged.

"They always pontificate a bit. I think it used to be worse. Some academics still want you to jump through hoops only because they had to jump through those same hoops."

"It's like some coming-of-age ceremonies in ancient cultures," I said.

She laughed. "You were lucky. You're so young they might have given you a really rough time."

I'd left my committee and called Denise. We ended up in a hangout near the university.

The bar had several rooms and served all kinds of goodies along with drinks. I saw a robowaiter take a communal plate of wriggling somethings to a table of Usk students. I knew some of them—the Usks, not the wrigglers—but it seemed like a private celebration too.

A band of Humans and Tali played happy music, and one Tali female didn't have a bad voice. The ballads she belted out almost seemed like military marches, but once I heard an old Earth tune I liked, "Stand by Me." Denise knew some of the musicians because, once when they were taking a break, she waved, and they waved back.

I'd turned my wi-fi implant off. Otherwise, the AI's translations of nearby conversations would have driven me crazy, and maybe it would have gone crazy trying to translate the scat singing of the Tali.

"I'm having second thoughts," I said looking at the happy Human faces. The ET faces were probably happy too, but it was often hard to read their body language. "It seems that my goals aren't normal ones. People gravitate to specialized occupations, to be sure, but I wonder how many put in the time to become an academic researcher."

"Even ETs cover a whole range of occupations. Not everyone wants to be an expert on something. You and I are weird in that sense. I'm more practical than you,

Asako, but it takes all kinds. You can't stay focused while having second thoughts. Get over them. You'll be specialized in something different from your parents' specialties, right?" I nodded. "So it's not that. You shouldn't try to please your parents anyway. You have to decide what you want to do and stick to it."

"Aren't you in that same boat?"

"And it has a leak in it." She laughed again. "There you have it. You're exactly where I am now." She thought a moment. "You can always go back and just work with the Fistians. You know, forget about the degree. Be their friends. Your friend Marcello sounds like a great guy."

I changed the topic slightly. "Are you going to stay on Sanctuary?"

"It depends. I'm working up to a decision. You know that."

"OK. I'll put it differently. Do you like Sanctuary?"

"I'd like to be on Novo Mondo more. If I stay with my group, though, we might be touring."

"That's a hard life. I heard Novo Mondo is a bustling place. Couldn't you just do local gigs there?"

"All TBD. We always come back to me. What about you? Do you like Sanctuary?"

"No. I'd rather be back on Hard Fist. Or New Haven, or Novo Mondo, or some of the less claustrophobic places in near-Earth space. I guess I'm a lucky researcher. The place I'll be doing my research is where I want to be, and it has a lot of wide open space."

"It's the place you know best. But don't let that restrict your curiosity. People who hang around the places where they're born don't have enough experiences that lead to wisdom."

"Wisdom? That's a curious word to use."

"The frontiers of your curiosity shouldn't be determined by a single place in the galaxy. But that's just my opinion." She indicated the rest of the room. "If you asked the people here, some would agree with me, others wouldn't. Even the ETs. We all have to make choices. Once made, though, they're sometimes hard to change."

"Are you getting drunk?"

"You have me at a disadvantage. You're not drinking alcohol."

I glanced at the bottle that was almost empty. "Maybe we'd better call it an evening."

Chapter Nine

I perhaps should say something more about the Interstellar Trade Union of Independent Planets. Not too long before the human survivors on Earth won back their planet from the Tali, both Humans and Rangers started discussing the need for a federation. Humans had stopped that collective intelligence called Swarm (a whole star cluster of linked intelligences) from cleansing near-Earth space of the Tali hordes, and Humans and Rangers were looking beyond the three original Human colonies to colonizing other worlds. The idea was to make official the nexus between the two groups of old friends and add to it colonies as they matured and wanted to participate in a more formal union.

It was all complicated by the limits of the FTL star drives. They were the fastest means of communication. I read once that it's comparable to what the Pony Express was on the North American continent on Earth. That reference was obscure for me, but I knew a pony was a kind of horse, so I thought communication that way would be a lot slower than via FTL. But I understood the limitations. It meant that ITUIP would never have quick communications to link its worlds together. But there would be trade, everyone hoped, and lots of it.

***

Sometime after that defeat of the Tali on Earth (they had already been limited to their original colonies, which included Earth and the Rangers' home world), an important meeting was called. It took several years to set it up. Its participants were delegations of Humans,

Rangers, and Tali. We hadn't met any other ETs at that time, but we would.

If I understand my history, creating ITUIP wasn't easy. There was still rancor between the initial group of Humans and Rangers and their old foes, the Tali, and vice versa. I can't imagine how they ever pulled it off.

I'd asked Dad2 about it one time when we were studying the whole process in school.

"Probably just luck," he'd said. "And we enjoy the benefits. Working together is a lot more productive than feuding."

That sounded a bit glib, and it didn't seem to jibe well with his perception of Fistians. I was pretty sure ITUIP wouldn't have existed if Mom and Dad2 had been at that convention. And the convention wouldn't have even been scheduled if Bobby's parents had any say.

But that taught me an important lesson: to get something accomplished, you not only need people who are motivated, you also need people who can make it happen. Maybe the creation of ITUIP was luck. I don't know.

It just seemed remarkable that it did happen, and ITUIP came into being.

***

Along with creating the federation, the ITUIP Protocol was developed. Not only did it discourage interference with other cultures that were already established, like on Hard Fist, it prohibited interference when those cultures didn't respect the basic freedoms and rights expressed in the ITUIP articles of federation. Colony worlds like Denise Amalfi's existed, many of them Human ones, where the majority of colonists were just plain crazy and dangerous. The Protocol called for a quarantine of those, and the SEB enforced it.

There were worlds under quarantine and there were worlds in near-Earth space that didn't belong to ITUIP. Trade didn't exist with the former, but it did with the latter. It was all a bit confusing. Most people, Humans and all ETs we've met, didn't pay much attention to it at all until there were crises. And because of the FTL limitation for communications, we often didn't learn about those crises until they were already happening or just part of an ever expanding history of near-Earth space. On a world like Hard Fist, it was more the latter.

ITUIP is often criticized, especially by those worlds that feel other worlds have obtained some advantage, but it seems to work, and the Protocol seems to be more positive than negative. That doesn't mean ITUIP worlds are utopias, of course. You have people like Bobby's parents in the best societies. At the time of signing the ITUIP articles, 40% of the Tali still yearned for the old days of the empire and were trapped in their psychological xenophobia. It was sobering that such things still existed.

Chapter Ten

There wasn't much ITUIP traffic to and from Hard Fist. I'd made the journey to and from Sanctuary on an SEB ship; I returned to do my thesis research the same way. Many people who never leave their home planets—that's most everyone on the known planets in near-Earth space—don't realize that subjective time onboard a starship can still seem long even though a person is effectively traveling many light-years by zipping through multiverses.

When they first developed the FTL drive on and around New Haven, they had setbacks. Space-time topologies are tricky in any multiverse, and some have to be avoided because ordinary matter can't exist there—maybe it has a different value of Planck's constant or the fine-structure constant, preponderance of antimatter over matter, and things like that. FTL is so tricky that a sophisticated AI has to handle everything.

I'd never been overly curious about those things. A starship is just a vehicle to me, something that takes me across the galaxy from point A to B. Much more interesting are the social dynamics onboard, which I'd wrongly chosen to ignore on my first two trips. Every starship is like a little tribe. I studied the *Balboa*'s crew on my trip home to practice my exosociological skills.

First, the crew was informal. I'd heard that on expensive cruise liners for tourists, the captain was always dressed in a crisp, white uniform, assuming he was a Human, which didn't have to be the case, of course, and he socialized a lot with tourists—the captain could also be a female. The crew was polished and civil too. For the

Balboa's crew, clothing was more for comfort, and they weren't too civil about letting me know I was more a nuisance for them, a kid who asked them far too many questions. I'd experienced that attitude on the first two trips and kept my mouth shut, but now I asked the questions. I'd never been timid, just practical, but now I felt I deserved some respect.

Most crewmembers still tried to ignore me; others tolerated me but didn't go out of their way to become friends. Of course, I could observe and analyze shipboard dynamics without receiving any answers to my questions, and that sometimes made them nervous too. I'd be nervous if I didn't feel like answering someone and that person still stared at me and tried to analyze the reason for my attitude. I recognized that, but I still didn't let up.

Second, graduates from universities and technical schools often had internships on SEB ships that would lead to secure jobs. My first two trips had no interns. Young people who chose that route had many motivations, but the overriding one for the more adventurous was to see as much of the galaxy as they could. That meant near-Earth space, of course, and a bit beyond—the galaxy is very big and it has many stars and planets. While every ITUIP world was near Earth, relatively speaking, near-Earth space also encompassed a lot of space and stars with planets, so it could interest the most adventurous.

Third, the food was terrible. That's how I met Doc. He caught me dumping half a plate of gunk the AI had served me into the recycling bin. The online menu had called it goulash, but it consisted of chunks of processed and fake protein (that ubiquitous soy-based stuff) swimming in a peculiar tasting pink sauce that looked a bit like bloody pus from a wound. *Ugh!* To be fair, I had no idea what the word goulash meant, but it had sounded intriguing and exotic. *Big mistake!* I had just decided to try to forget the whole experience as soon as possible and go hungry when Doc walked into the room.

Doc wasn't a doc yet. He was an intern for the ship's Tali medical officer. His curly hair, shiny brown skin but lighter than Denise's, and wide smile won me over instantly. He looked like a healthy Human male—not unusual for medical personnel, I suppose—and would have looked fabulous in one of those starched cruise ship uniforms. Instead, he was dressed in only shorts and sandals and needed a shave. He reminded me of the male Human scientists on Hard Fist in that way, except they usually wore shirts.

***

"You have to train our stupid AI to serve what you like," Doc said, eying me with his big, bright eyes. Even from a few meters away, I felt I could get lost in them. He had long, handsome lashes too. *Why can't I have ones like that?* Genetic engineering didn't seem to attend to details like eyelashes!

"I haven't had a decent meal since I left Hard Fist," I said. "I can hardly wait to return home. At least there I can figure out what they're serving."

"We have two stops at planets before that, so you'll have to wait for your home-cooked food." He touched the menu on the screen embedded in the table. "See the icon marked 'Your Recipe?' If you push that, you can give the AI a personal recipe that it will repeat *ad nauseum* as long as you ask it to do so."

He explained that a recipe was an algorithm for preparing a person's special dish or drink. News to me. I knew how to boil water and allow for different atmospheric pressures while doing so. That was about it. And I was regretting that no one had explained this on my way back and forth to Sanctuary before. I'd also hated the food then.

"I was just choosing from a ready menu. I'm terrible at computer code."

"Here's an example." He pressed the icon. "Alfred, record recipe named 'havenberry hangover.'" Doc rattled off directions for a mixed drink. Alfred, the AI made it, and the concoction popped out in a recess in the wall at one end of the table. Doc handed it to me. "Now any time you want a havenberry hangover, he'll make it to perfection. Your drink will lack a living barkeep's touch on habited planets, but it's handy here."

I sniffed at it. "Fermented juice?"

"No, that's the vodka. You're just getting the vapors. Vodka is tasteless and ideal for mixing drinks. And it's inexpensive. In this drink, it's mixed with the havenberry juice. I doubt the latter is real because it's an expensive delicacy. The vodka is distilled from real potatoes, though."

"What's a potato?"

"A tuber from Earth. It's a popular source of starch on many planets."

"Not on Hard Fist." I took a sip. "I'm not good with alcohol." I put the drink down. Some things were best left for grown-ups. The Fistians' fermented drinks I'd innocently sampled had proven that on several occasions.

"Take your time." Shook my head and smiled. "Alfred, make me a grilled ham and cheese sandwich." A few seconds later, he handed me a paper plate. "Eat that. Fake smoked ham and Swiss cheese, but tasty nonetheless. It's not good to drink liquor on an empty stomach, and you'll probably like this sandwich better than the goulash."

I pushed the drink aside and worked on the sandwich.

***

Doc and I hit it off. His real name was Santiago Regenbogen. I could understand why people called him Doc. He skipped the Kobayashi and called me Asako. We had no professional interests in common, just a lot of hormonal attraction, what people often called chemistry. Bobby faded from my mind; Santiago occupied my thoughts when I wasn't polishing more detailed plans for writing my thesis—I'd had some ideas since defending my project.

He began spending his off-duty hours with me, and I used that time to take a break from brain-strain. He was a lot of fun. On the second stop we made, a beautiful planet named Nirvana, he received some planet-side leave, so I went down with him on the shuttle to explore a bit.

Rangers outnumber Humans and other intelligent lifeforms ten to one there, but some enterprising Humans and Tali had set up businesses renting water sports equipment to rich Human tourists who frequented the planet as a vacation spot. Some people have far too much money, I suppose, so there would always be other people to encourage them to spend it, and that was the main industry on the planet Nirvana.

One cruise liner was parked in orbit, in fact. Many passengers were touring the planet and using those rentals. I didn't like any of the tourists because they seemed shallow and overly needy and spoiled, but most seemed harmless enough. Maybe the neediness was due to being on a cruise that was their first trip into space. Considering their luxurious accommodations I'd heard about, they had no right to complain. They should have mine on the *Balboa!*

"Can't we find somewhere more peaceful?" I said to Doc as we sat on stools at a beach hangout sipping havenberry juice made from berries harvested right on Nirvana. It was an important business for the local Rangers. Why didn't the *Balboa* take advantage of that and stock up on the tasty juice? I supposed it was the cost. Doc had treated me, but each glass was a week's pay for the intern; I saw the price on the short menu posted on the rustic walls. I felt guilty.

"You find the ship claustrophobic and this planet just the opposite?"

Here he's analyzing me, the exosociologist! "They all seem so self-centered," I said, "and there are too many of them. It's a lot of people packed into small spaces that bothers me. As big as the planet is, this little tourist town is overcrowded."

"Because it's nearer the spaceport. I've been here before. It's better when there are no cruise liners in port. With just one, the town of Good Karma Bay becomes overpopulated. That's why Rangers mostly avoid it." He thought a moment. "I have a solution."

We rented a water-sled from a corpulent Human who looked like a picture I'd once seen of Santa Claus, a mythical Earth figure who supposedly gave presents to kids once every year. Don't ask me why. Kids should have presents all year long. This man only wore a red speedo, though, and his beard was a bit short and still had some black in it. Couldn't figure him out. Why didn't he trim down? Maybe he was sick?

We were soon skipping over the waves on our way to a deserted island in the Good Karma archipelago that the fellow renting the sled assured us had the best sandy beaches in the area. Doc had been there before, so he knew the recommendation was sound.

"Nirvana's a watery world like New Haven where I grew up," Doc said as we dragged the water-sled above the tide line on one of the small island's beaches. "If you get away from all the tourists, it could be a twin. Right now the only real industry here is tourism."

"Even for Rangers?"

"Not exactly, because they're mostly just living a traditional and carefree Ranger life, enjoying all this water, and helping to produce services and things the tourists yearn for."

Farther up the beach, we found some trees, strange ones with rough bark and purple leaves, but they were big fellows and offered plenty of shade. They reminded me of trees on Hard Fist that grew tall because they had to compete with their rainforest brethren.

"What are you doing?" I said when he started removing his clothes.

"They're all wet. If we spread them out, they'll dry."

"Is that your only intention?" I said with a smile.

"Maybe not. I like you a lot, Asako."

My first real love affair started that way as I willingly let an older fellow seduce me. I thought it was about time, it seemed natural, and I liked Doc a lot too.

***

Doc had originally wanted to have a practice on Novo Mondo because he'd learned that planet in the Tau Ceti system had the largest population and it was an unusual mix of Humans and various groups of ETs, with none of them in the majority. In other words, he could practice medicine on many different intelligent beings.

But then the space exploration bug bit him. He'd decided he wanted to be in situations where he'd be forced to figure out how to care for a previously unknown intelligent lifeform. The Space Exploration Bureau (SEB) was the obvious choice for doing that, so he opted to become an intern, a decision not popular with his physician father. For Doc, it wasn't about making a lot of money; it was about adventures to be had working at the frontiers of medicine on frontier planets.

It seemed impossible we could have a life together under those circumstances. I'd already imagined a full life for myself on Hard Fist and similar frontier planets, long sojourns for studying different ET cultures. He seemed to be more of a gypsy nomad—I'd read about them in my school's history courses, and the words seemed to describe his outlook on life well...and my infatuation with him.

I suspected reckless infatuation destroys a lot of relationships when the infatuation wears off and reality sets in as the dyad or triad gets down to the details of living together. I wondered if Doc would be happy on Hard Fist, or if I could be happy with him on a developed planet like Novo Mondo.

I'd already learned from Doc details about how the anatomy of intelligent lifeforms works together with evolution. Most were bipeds like Humans and Tali, and had hands because they used tools. Some, like Fistians and Rangers, weren't bipeds but still had serviceable hands. Procreation depended on anatomy too and influenced social organization and culture. There were hive-like social organizations like the Arlamati. The most unusual intelligent lifeforms were collective ones that ranged from colonies of small animals bonding together to planet-wide ones like Singer, a worldwide fish-like school that had cured Swarm's insanity. Of course,

Swarm was the biggest collective lifeform we'd met so far.

But Doc wasn't just interested in anatomy. He was interested in anything that related to determining the necessary medical protocols—anatomy, afflictions, infections, biochemistry, diet, and genetic carriers and traits, for example. I was more interested in how all those things related to cultures.

None of these differences would have bothered me— some argue that dyads and triads are more stable if interests complement each other and don't overlap much—but being separated for long periods would. I realized life could present me a series of problems, but I didn't know if I could solve this one regarding my future with Doc.

Of course, I came to my senses and decided I was egotistical and selfish even to think Doc wanted *any kind* of permanent relationship. I also decided just to enjoy the time I had with him and worry about our future together later. But he at least distracted me from my more immediate problem: how to learn enough about Fistians to write a research thesis!

***

Doc also participated in another aspect of my extracurricular education beyond learning about erogenous zones. When we returned to the *Balboa* after our little holiday on Nirvana, he educated me about some dangers associated with spacewalks—not very practical for someone planning a life of planet hopping, but an interesting adventure.

Many Humans in those three original colony ships that ended up at New Haven, Novo Mundo, and Sanctuary were Spacers, a name given to them in the home system. Their opposites were Downies, the stay-at-home types who lived on Earth. I'd be a Downy staying on Hard Fist, for example. Even the Lunar and Mars colonists were often called Downies, but they were also Spacers in the sense that they had learned to live off Earth. It was natural that the first interstellar explorers came from that hardy stock.

Balboa had its departure delayed because they were waiting for some new filters for the environmental system. That surprised me because it seemed odd to find such replacement parts on Nirvana, but Doc explained that the planet had to be ready to repair the many cruise ships that arrived almost weekly. Those parts were interchangeable; cruise liners just needed more of them than SEB's starships.

I was also surprised when Doc invited me on that spacewalk.

"You mean, go outside the ship?"

"That's exactly what I mean. I have to check on a little experiment my boss and I are running. There's no hurry to do so, but I might as well see if there's any change because we're stuck here for a bit longer."

I hoped he meant "stuck in orbit." *If he means, stuck with me, I'll never forgive him!* Paranoia for not having many romantic interludes in my young life? That thought bothered me even more!

"What's the experiment?"

"We're trying to prove spores from one planet can survive a trip in hard vacuum to begin life on another world."

"Doesn't the ship leave ordinary space when it goes FTL? Space in another metaverse could bias your results, to say the least."

"That's perceptive, but the AI remotely seals the experiment up just before going FTL. About 40% of any journey is done in normal space."

I knew that. "Any conclusions yet?"

"Not solid ones. They are surviving, though, for the most part."

"If they do survive, what does it mean?"

"Only that it's possible that life in one place can end up starting it in another."

"But all the intelligent lifeforms we've encountered look different."

"Primitive spores going from planet to planet could evolve differently on each planet."

"Meaning some spores from billions of years ago spawned all life?"

"Maybe in regions a galaxy, or an entire galaxy. I doubt it works from galaxy to galaxy."

"Hmm. It's still hard to believe."

"It's just an experiment. We don't have to believe it; just collect the data." Doc smiled. "Have you ever been in space?" I shook my head. "Then go with me."

So he gave me this idea to go on a spacewalk with him to pay tribute to my Spacer ancestors. It sounded safe enough. I'd be tethered to Doc. And we wouldn't be floating around either because the ship's artificial gravity pointed down toward the ship's center. Considering what had happened on Nirvana, the spacewalk seemed a bit celebratory too. A tip o' my hat—rather, space helmet— to that wonderful planet where I was seduced by a fantastic guy.

The spacesuit adjusted itself to my body, and I caught Doc's appreciative eye. He'd seen me naked, so what was the big deal? Together with the breathing unit and helmet, the suit looked almost like the diving suits I'd seen in Nirvana's rental shops. I didn't feel at all clumsy.

"Come along, my Ninja warrior."

I was still wondering what that meant as we exited the space lock. I'd have to look it up. I followed Doc across the hull to the experimental site. As we shuffled along, I noticed small knobs spaced periodically on the hull. I asked Doc about them.

"Most starships have shields. *Balboa* has no offensive weapons, but the shield offers some defense if we're ever attacked. Nowadays that would most likely be a pirate attack, but you never know."

"There are pirates?" The word almost seemed foreign to me.

"SEB ships go to some out-of-the-way places, Asako. Life is ubiquitous in the galaxy, and sometimes it's hostile, as the Tali and Usks once were. SEB's standard tactic is shields up, flee the solar system, and go FTL as fast as possible. We'd definitely write that solar system off in that case."

It dawned on me that life in the Space Exploration Bureau could be dangerous and not just a scientific walk in the park. I thought about that until we arrived at the experiment. Watched him check the spores and download some data to the ship's AI.

"That's all there is to it," he said.

"Seems more like exobiological research rather than medical."

"The old Tali does more than just medicine." He took up the slack in my tether. "Ready?"

"For what?"

"We've walked around almost fifty percent of the sphere that's the ship's hull. Look up."

I did…and I saw Nirvana looming over me. That's when I lost my breakfast. So much for my tip o' the hat! I thought I was going to smother in my own vomit, but that smart spacesuit had safety features, and one was designed just for such situations. It sucked up the vomit, but the stench remained.

Back inside the lock, I was embarrassed when Doc helped me out of the suit.

"You look a bit pale, Asako. I'm sorry. I shouldn't have asked you to come. But planets look so beautiful from low orbit. Especially Nirvana."

"I guess it was beautiful." I tapped my head. "In here." I rubbed my stomach. "Not in here."

"Sometimes it requires some practice. I'm truly sorry."

"Not your fault. But you won't get me to do it again."

So much for my Spacer genes. Hard Fist was looking even better now. At least my feet would be on solid ground!

By the time we finally arrived there, life had become very confusing for me. I thought I loved Doc in spite of the spacewalk and in spite of our differences. I understood Denise's dilemma completely. Doc seemed confused too.

Our lengthy goodbye kisses received some hard looks from Mom and Dad2.

PART III:
FISTIANS
AND
HUMANS

A.B. CAROLAN

Chapter Eleven

And so it was a little more than a Standard year after I'd journeyed to Sanctuary for the second time in different starships when I left my parents' cabin in the science compound and walked toward the Fistian village, breaking with Human tradition yet again. Not much had changed. I was still the only Human to visit their village as far as I knew, at least intentionally and with the purpose of speaking to Fistians. That's me, so-called Human genius and epitome of young brashness.

I took pride in those labels, though. I didn't believe the genius label, of course, but all the professors on Sanctuary had thought I was another Einstein. I knew better. First, Einstein was a physicist. I knew that because the Humans' AI was named after him, and, as a curious kid, I'd researched what he had done long ago. Second, I had proof I was no genius. If Marcello hadn't saved me from that drooler, my stupidity would now be known far and wide…and then forgotten, because everyone is embarrassed by stupidity, and many scientists would just have said, "Good thing she didn't leave any offspring," or something worse. Of course, I wouldn't care much being dead, but now I had things to do and needed to stay safe on Hard Fist so I could get on doing them. I'd never told my parents about that drooler, just that I'd had an accident and broke my leg and Marcello had found me.

While Human interest in native Fistians hadn't changed, Hard Fist had in that one long year. Not far from the scientists' compound that had been my home for thirteen years was a new mining camp. It was part of a mining boomlet (there were five other camps) due to the discovery of deposits of rare earth minerals by one of our exogeologists. While my birthplace, now called Brainsville by miners, was quiet and contemplative, I'd heard the mining town called Middle Finger was noisy and rowdy. The prospectors had come up with both names—the scientists and engineers had nothing to do with them. The miners in the camp were rumored to be even more hostile to native Fistians than scientists and engineers in Brainsville.

After that period of intensive study on Sanctuary, I was back on Hard Fist ready to do research and write my thesis—it would be my ticket to an advanced degree. With much work and Marcello's help, I hoped to become eventually Dr. Kobayashi, exosociologist from Hard Fist and the galaxy's leading expert on native Fistians, at least in that small part of the galaxy near Earth touched by Humans. I assumed the rest of the galaxy didn't yet know about either Fistians or Humans.

You might wonder why Human scientists didn't have other exosociologists or exoanthropologists studying Fistians (yeah, the latter professional name doesn't make sense unless Humans living on other planets are being studied). Originally there were two persons with those professional credentials among the scientists. They had both died before I was born. The first had too close an encounter with a drooler, the first such Human-drooler encounter, in fact. The other was buried somewhere in a rock slide under tons of boulders. They'd never been replaced, so now I had the job by default. I hoped to last a bit longer than they had.

***

At the Fistian village's outskirts, the wide, packed-dirt path had morphed into worn cobblestones. I'd walked over them before, but now it occurred to me that I had no idea how old they were—yet another piece of evidence that my knowledge of Fistian history was severely limited. The road soon became a wider thoroughfare, widening as it moved through the village until it turned into a plaza.

I still had the wi-fi unit they'd implanted in the right side of my head on Sanctuary. By then I was used to it. Most people, even ETs, had one, but I hadn't as a kid on Hard Fist. It came in handy now. Before I'd left Sanctuary, I'd upgraded the memory in the unit so I could record my observations about Fistian culture and download them when I was within range to connect with Einstein. I'd maintained a running commentary with the unit as I'd approached the village.

That technology had first appeared mid-21st century on Earth and had become the standard tool for communications between intelligent lifeforms. It had grown out of cochlear implant technologies. It also was an example of my attitude toward technology: I didn't have to understand it 100%, just enough to use it. We call our societies technological ones now, but so many of us are technological savages as far as our understanding of how things work goes.

But, at the same time, we become more specialized. Robots and androids do much of the physical work on advanced planets, and AIs take care of all the services and coordinate everything. Humans and ETs alike still didn't seem to have more free time, though. Everyone always seemed to be busy with something. Sometimes I thought technology had enslaved us. Marcello's people seemed to have avoided that.

The Fistians weren't a technological society, but the village had always seemed busy. Now it seemed deserted.

I didn't snoop around. Fistians were trusting, so I could just walk into a dwelling to see if anyone was there inside, but I respected their privacy. I did look around, though, and wondered about my timing. I remembered the place as bustling, filled with Fistians who usually scurried around and ignored me as they went about their business.

The short hair on the nape of my neck bristled. *Did something happen to my friends?* My parents had said nothing about tragic events affecting the village. *But maybe they didn't hear about them? Or worse, didn't care.* I couldn't imagine what could wipe out an entire village. *Maybe droolers did hunt in packs and a pack of the brutes had attacked the village?* Yet everywhere I looked, I saw signs of the organized Fistian home life I knew—an orderly village baking in the strong sun.

Running perpendicular to the road I had come in on and meeting it at the plaza was another road of equal width. I looked down the east end and saw foothills and far-away mountains—the high country. Down the west end I could see in the distance a beautiful beach that curved around a huge bay where the wide river that flowed close to the village entered the sea. Both our science station and this Fistian village were just inland from this bay at a prudent distance to avoid high tides caused by Big Fellow and other nearby satellites, companions of Hard Fist. Middle Finger could be found up the coast and also inland, but it seemed to be covered by a smoky haze.

Where is everybody? How am I going to study these people if I can't find them?

***

I once had taken a tour of Hard Fist in a helicopter. Dad2 thought it would be fun for me. I remembered some of it, but I had been very young. Brainsville and

Marcello's village were on the largest continent, really not much more than a large island. There were many continents and islands scattered all over the satellite and almost all of them had no Humans on them except when some scientist like my mother or father visited as part of her or his research.

Fistian villages could be found all over the satellite, though, but it was hard to estimate how many Fistians were in each one. Marcello's was more important to me because I'd been visiting it and no other for a long time, but from the air the others had looked to have about the same number of dwellings. I had no idea how many Fistians lived in each one, though, because I'd never been in a Fistian dwelling. Again, something I didn't know about the Fistians; I had to remedy that.

In some villages, I had seen Fistians milling around. None of them waved at us, although a few looked skyward at the silent intruder in their airspace. Did those Fistians even know what Humans looked like?

Most villages were also built on rivers not far from where they emptied into the ocean. They seemed to be carefully planned communities with dwellings of uniform size. I saw no sign of community houses or other buildings that might be used for large gatherings of a bureaucratic or religious nature. I saw some cultivated fields but concluded that Fistians lived mostly off the land. *Are they primitives? Or are they post-technological?* Two more questions to be answered in my thesis. It could be either one, but the well-constructed dwellings told me they weren't nomads.

On that trip around Hard Fist where we made several stops when Dad2 decided he needed to take measurements or collect samples, I also had concluded that Fistians took care of their environment. Many square miles of lush plains and pristine rainforests indicated respect for their world. And Hard Fist is a beautiful world—a raw, primitive world to be sure, with dangers amidst all that beauty, but a world that enjoyed extraordinary care from its intelligent lifeform, the Fistians.

It was humbling experience for me. I knew from my school and my own perusal of computer files about Human history on Earth and elsewhere that we didn't have such a good track record on environmental issues. Many species had gone extinct on Earth, for example, even before the Tali started to mold Earth's environment to match their home world's.

Maybe Humans had a lot to learn from Fistians.

***

The long walk from the science station had left me coated in perspiration that couldn't evaporate in the humid air. I could run a finger down my cheeks and arms and push it off. Even the slightest breeze would have been comforting; there was none. I could feel the heat in the cobblestones and wondered if my synthetic boots would soon melt.

A few things had changed. In the center of the plaza, there was now a circular stone cistern that looked new. It had a radius of about ten meters and a depth of maybe a meter. The water was covered with pond scum, but I was thirsty. I figured if there was anything bad in the water, they'd have a cure for it back at the science station.

I sat on the cistern's ledge, leaned over, cupped my hands, and scooped up liquid. It was slimy, but it was wet. *Will the slime make me sick?* I cursed my stupidity for not bringing a canteen of purified water. Or filters for any water I found.

"You might want to go easy on that," said a voice behind me.

I turned and faced a large Fistian, noting the use of Standard. I didn't know much Fistian, of course. *Would I need to learn it for the thesis?* It always had seemed to be a complicated language where snorts and whistles and body movement seemed to contribute as much as sounds that could only be words. None of them wore translator units that could help with translations either. I suppose my unit could have contained a fairly large vocabulary, but that wouldn't help a Fistian translate from standard. And I was certain no Human had studied the Fistian language. Marcello learned languages so easily that I'd never needed to know Fistian, but this Fistian's knowledge of Standard seemed unusual.

"It's OK to drink it, right?"

I was wondering if there was some religious significance to the new cistern, although I couldn't remember any details about Fistian religion. In fact, I'd never discussed religion with Marcello. *And you want to write an exosociological thesis?* I thought. I seemed to remember references from him about the sky, ground, and water, but I'd have to do better than that.

"Of course. The animals drink from it all the time. It's one of our new wells. But we don't drink this water. It's what you Humans call unsanitary. High bacterial content."

I was confirming with each word that our common stereotype of prehistoric Fistians was completely wrong. *New wells? Bacterial content?* I doubted that prehistoric Humans knew anything about wells and bacteria.

I stood and realized how large this Fistian female was. Large means like larger than one of those huge carriage horses you'd see if you ever studied Earth animals.

Dwarfed me completely. Could crush me as easily as she brushed off flies with her tail either by sitting on me or squeezing me with those big hands—arms the length of my legs, hands as big as two of mine, with long, delicate fingers. Expressive eyes set apart in a large forehead, ears rotating to capture sound in the same way our com antennas snooped out the electronic environment—of course, that wasn't needed much on Hard Fist.

I wiped off my hands on my pants and stuck one out in greeting. "I'm Asako Kobayashi, from the Humans' science station."

"Yes, I remember you," said the Fistian, bowing her head a bit and grasping my hand. "You don't remember me, it seems. You called me Mama Dora. I'm the clan mother." She had my hand in both of hers and pumped it up and down. "We have always called you First Born."

"First Born?" I said, hiding my embarrassment for not remembering her, but I'd spent a lot more time with Marcello than any other Fistian.

"The first Human child born on Hard Fist," said Mama Dora.

"You look so old," I said. *Possible error?* Some intelligent beings didn't like to be reminded of their age...or youth, for that matter, as in my case.

Her laugh, more of a bellow, echoed off the walls of nearby buildings. Made me recall Marcello's laugh. Her eyebrows danced up and down, also reflecting humor. "Before, when we first met, I was old. Now I am older still, but somedays I feel ancient."

I shrugged. "My father says that you are only as old as you act."

"Your father is a wise Human. I would like to meet him."

Yeah, sure, maybe during the next glacial period of this satellite? "Back to the water. Where can I find some clean water?" That seemed a little whiny, but it was a way to get back in her good graces. She was clan mother, after all. *Doesn't that mean she mothers everyone in the village?* Seemed like a good opportunity to find out.

She raised her heavy eyebrows again above those expressive eyes. I had learned long ago from Marcello that this was the Fistian smile. "Follow me, little one. If you want to study us, you must see how we live."

She trotted off, her padded hoofs silent on the cobblestones. *Not too much like a centaur,* I thought, as I struggled to keep up. Of course, I had no idea how a centaur walked! *And how does she know I want to study them? I hadn't even told Marcello that, not knowing how he'd react to being an object of study. I'd only said I was going to Sanctuary to study.*

Chapter Twelve

We didn't go far.

We turned off the main thoroughfare and entered a small circle of buildings. In the center of the circle, there was another smaller cistern. Dora stopped in front of one building and pushed aside a beaded curtain that served as a door.

"Welcome to my home," she said, bowing and motioning for me to enter.

I bowed too, went inside, and she followed.

I had never been in a Fistian home before. Marcello and I had always played in the streets of the village or in the wild lands outside it. It wasn't like anyone had prohibited or anything. I'd just wanted to respect their privacy. You only enter someone's home when you're invited—I now had the implicit invitation.

The building was about seven meters by seven meters in floor area and that was divided into four areas—I wouldn't exactly call them rooms. One area seemed to be for cooking, judging by the utensils and Fistian fruits and vegetables sitting on a counter. The entrance area where we were standing had cushions placed around the floor. I couldn't see what function the other two areas had, but everything looked austere and functional, not unlike my parents' abode.

There was a door in the back as well as the front, both covered with those beads. The windows were open and not covered. The roof seemed to be made from sheaves of leaves taken from the tall trees so common in the rainforest.

The construction material for the walls and interior divisions seemed to be granite. Dad2 had told me once that there had been a debate whether granite is an igneous or metamorphic rock. I couldn't remember if someone had won that debate—my five-year-old eyes were probably glazing over—but I'm guessing on Hard Fist granite was igneous with all the volcanic activity around. I noticed there was no mortar between the stone blocks, yet they fit tightly together implying exact tolerances.

"Please sit down and I will bring you water."

I sat down in a lotus position on one of the floor cushions. Dora, after handing me a bowl of water, sat down on another—better said, she parked her rear end on it while supporting her upper body with her forelimbs. That left her hands free.

"Where is everyone?" I said, after emptying the bowl and wiping my mouth with the back of my hand. "And thanks for the water, by the way."

"Our ancestors provide well for us on Hard Fist," she said. "There is no need to thank me. And, to answer your question, I believe we are in what you Humans might call nap time." She gestured around her home. "You have your noisy machines to cool yourself at this time of day. We simply sleep through it. But one of us is always awake to stand guard and sound the alarm if necessary. You never know when a drooler might decide to wander into the village." Her eyebrows danced. Figured Marcello had probably told her about my encounter with that young beast. I felt embarrassed. "Today it's my turn."

"And who determines whose turn it is?"

"I do. But even the clan mother must take her turn. That's only fair, and it's our tradition. The ancestors might be upset if we broke with tradition."

***

I looked around the tiny house. It was difficult to determine if there were others living there.

"Are you alone? Do you have children?"

Again the raised eyebrows. "How can I be alone if I live here in the village? And yes, I do have children. They are all much older than you are. Many generations live together in peace in our village and elsewhere."

I thought for a bit. "How old are you?"

"That's difficult to say in your units of time. I was born in another village over 1000 turns of Big Fellow around our sun ago."

Because that period was almost half a Standard Year, that made her over 500 years old. I was impressed. At that time, Humans were just colonizing New Haven, Sanctuary, and Novo Mondo. We hadn't even met our first ETs on New Haven.

"Have you always lived this idyllic lifestyle?"

"I don't understand."

"Has the village always been this small?"

"When a village grows too large, some of us move somewhere else and create a new one. I've participated in several such splits, but only this last time did I become clan mother. But come, I will present you to the other villagers."

***

I had begun to hear noise. We returned to the central plaza where it seemed that a raucous party was now in full swing. A small group of musicians was playing a lively tune. One played the melody, theme, riff, or whatever you might call it, on some kind of flute. A musician with a long four-stringed instrument accompanied, maintaining a dirge-like background that contrasted with that melody. Another Fistian was chanting or singing. Others were stomping around in what could only be considered a dance. They were surrounded by about one hundred others, sitting on their hindquarters and clapping.

Fistians didn't seem to have professional musicians like my friend Denise wanted to be. Some musicians in that village group were better than others, but they all seemed to enjoy participating. It seemed spontaneous with heads nodding and marking time because sometimes the clapping got out of sync. The dancing was spontaneous too. Some would stop, some would start—a chaotic but entertaining performance. The rhythms were complicated and intoxicating, and even old adults as large as Mama Dora or larger became nimble and inventive.

"Market day," said Mama Dora, stopping before me after stomping around and tossing her mane. "And excess energy from taking a nap. It's still hot, though, so they won't be doing this for too long. I for one am too old to continue." She was panting. "Evenings are more festive because it's already cooling down."

Merchants selling their meat and vegetable produce in the market place added to the din. Some also beat on pots and pans, a few in time with the music, but most not. I couldn't recognize the origin of the big slabs of meat—I supposed there were many animal species Humans didn't know about yet, although Mom always seemed to be busy classifying and cataloging them.

A slightly smaller Fistian approached Mama Dora, made a bow, and waved a hand at me. I couldn't follow what was asked.

"This is—" Mama Dora thought a moment. "—your old friend whom you called Marcello. He wants to know if you remember him."

Again, I was embarrassed. I hadn't recognized my old friend. What a difference a few Standard years make! He was always big, but now he was bigger. I thought I still looked the same, but Marcello had changed even more than Mama Dora. I gave him a big hug.

"You were gone a long time," he said.

I took what he'd said as a rebuke. "I told you it would be a long time. I thought it would even be longer. I was lucky. My parents drove me nuts adding to my schooling here, but it paid off on Sanctuary. I was able to pass many competency tests at the university. I'm still sorry it took so long."

"You could have written."

I studied him for a few beats. His eyebrows were dancing a lot, the equivalent of a silent laugh or smile. *Is he teasing me?*

"Nothing goes faster than our starships."

Now his eyebrows danced double time to the music. He hugged me, this time longer. "Of course not. I understand. I am making a joke." He backed off and stretched his arms wide. "I'm full width and length now. Almost grown." He then pointed both index fingers towards my chest. "You are now a mature Human female."

I knew I was turning red. *Let's get off the exobiology stuff, Marcello.*

"You have to tell me all that's happened since I left."

Mama Dora pushed us toward the perimeter of the plaza. "Go. Talk. It's too noisy here."

I realized we'd been almost yelling. I hesitated for a moment but then swung on top of Marcello, grabbing his mane. It was fuller now, but it felt good and a bit like coming home.

Chapter Thirteen

It was almost like old times as Marcello galloped through the forest and I hung on tight. I weighed more but Marcello was stronger too. I almost felt happy to see blister vines.

We stopped at a little meadow beside a large lake. Stopped is not an apt description, though—Marcello just galloped right into the lake. The water pushed me off him. I didn't mind. It was cool and refreshing compared to the humid air.

"There are many more Humans here now," said Marcello. He was treading water with his four legs while stretching out his long arms to float. "The miners like us even less than your parents' people."

I was floating on my back. My hair spread out in the water and framed my face. On Sanctuary you don't have many outside activities. I'd swum in Lonely Swimmer's tank, but that wasn't the same as swimming on Hard Fist. I liked either fresh water or ocean water—both were refreshing in the heat and humidity because the cold nights kept the waters cool. I was enjoying Fistian sunshine and my impromptu bath much more than swimming in a tank on Sanctuary. And I could swim much better now. I swam to the center of the pond and back.

"Have they done anything bad to your people?" I said.

"Nothing more than shoo us out of town. Why are they like that? Some of us thought they might be interested in our fresh produce. We do have some nice crops, you know. They don't grow their own food like your parents' people."

"Because I don't know them, I can't make any comments with confidence. But I know their type. They probably are only interested in making their ore quotas. People can become very narrow-minded when they're prospecting." I didn't like the way the discussion was going. "So, did you miss me?"

"I can only say this is the most fun I've had in some time. What about you?"

"The same. How did Mama Dora know I'm going to study you and your people?"

"The ancestors told us, of course."

That was the very first time I'd heard anything so direct about the ancestors from Marcello. I recalled that Mama Dora had mentioned them. Try as I might, I couldn't get him to elaborate.

Again, I had to change the subject.

***

I went back to the Fistian village every day during the next week. All of the villagers were welcoming and chatty, now as curious about me as I was about them. They no longer ignored me. I was mingling with them. *Are they proud that they are the ones I'm studying?* But then I thought of the miners. *Or are they happy that little Asako treats them in a dignified way?*

I changed my views about the clan structure, now seeing it as a much more complicated social organization than I'd first imagined. Each village was a clan, and when it became too big, the village split and another village came into existence and another clan formed. It worked the other way too. Because of this process, Fistians in one village often had connections with many people in other villages.

Many discussions meandered their way around to where some Fistian mentioned ancestors. When I pressed for details, they would detour me, just like Marcello. It was like running a maze where there was no solution to find your way through it all the way to the end. I knew I could never write a thesis about Fistians without understanding their religion. It had to involve some kind of ancestor worship. From my studies, I knew that was indicative of a primitive social structure. But I wondered how the Fistians could be primitive if they'd been masters of Hard Fist for so long. Mama Dora wasn't nearly the oldest Fistian.

One conversational detour I had to make often had to do with differences between Brainsville and Middle Finger. I could tell them a lot about Brainsville. I couldn't tell them much about Middle Finger. I'd never been there. If only to answer their questions, I decided I'd have to visit. Considering my age, I didn't expect an invitation, so I decided my visit would have to be uninvited. I didn't even think of any possible risk.

Any group has its own subcultural characteristics. I expected the mining camp to have many strange quirks, probably more typical of new colonial settlements with a rigid, focused social structure than the loose structure found in Brainsville where everyone was engrossed in their own research activities. I'd experienced some variety in social organization on Sanctuary, but it too was unusual and probably atypical. I'd studied situations in other ITUIP worlds using computer files, but I would have to work with Einstein and brush up on those just to provide context for my study of the miners.

That made me recall Lonely Swimmer's tale about his studies of the Tali and Usks. How I admired that old Ranger and her ability to relate to different ETs. The Rangers had essentially approached Humans, not the other way around. They were naturally curious about everything.

***

I walked toward the coast following well-trodden paths along the river laid down by generations of Fistians. The heat was oppressive, but I enjoyed the walk. This was my home. I'd felt claustrophobic in Sanctuary's domes. Here it was just me and Hard Fist. Big Fellow had paled to the point where it was almost invisible in the intense blue sky. Creatures from the rainforest called out to me. I tried to call back, mimicking them the best I could. Some responded; others became quiet.

At one point a group of those large insects flew past, heading toward the ocean. They ignored me except for one that was lagging. It hovered around me as if it were studying a strange animal it had never seen before. I studied it as it studied me with those four large eyes. I was wondering how intelligent they were. I was also thinking that any aeronautical engineer would probably wonder how the insects flew. The wings seemed to be rotating; I recalled the drones some scientists at Brainsville used. The mandibles looked dangerous and the feet had little claws. Was it a carnivore? I'd have to ask Mom. The lagging one then sped off to join its friends. If they were carnivorous, maybe I was lucky they didn't recognize me as food. If that whole group had attacked me, I might have been a goner.

Passing through some low hills before reaching the coast, I turned northward toward Middle Finger along a trail that paralleled those hills. It climbed to an overlook at the beginning of one of those fissures filled with lava. In the distance I could see the waterfall of ocean water plummeting into the magma, sending steam soaring into the air. The fissure was a red slash perpendicular to the coast.

At that point I found some kind of Fistian shrine made of igneous rocks—not granite but something else. Dad2 would have known. I'd been there before with Marcello, but it was like I was seeing it for the first time. I remembered Marcello saying it had been built out of respect for their planet, a thank you to Hard Fist for giving them life and a home.

I could understand the sentiment looking across the canopy of rainforest to the ocean cliffs and farther out to sea. Unlike the miners, I had no desire to change anything. This was my land as much as the land of the Fistians.

Chapter Fourteen

Middle Finger made Brainsville look like Nirvana. I felt a bit apprehensive about being alone as I walked into a dirty camp that made me feel even less clean than that dip in the slime Marcello had subjected me to so long ago. As soon as I entered the tent town, I sensed miners' eyes undressing me. I suppose that's typical—most Humans in their situation males who were alone without their dyads or triads to accompany them, if they were part of one. But I didn't yet have the complete physical attributes of a mature Human female in spite of Marcello's comments, so the ogling seemed a bit perverted. I filed my observation away, swallowed my fear, and continued my exploration of the mining camp.

After scouting it out a bit with the secondary motivation of trying to find a place to pee, I saw an old man without a shirt and a curly beard hanging down to his belly button beckon to me from in front of a tent that had seen better days. Compared to other ogling miners I'd spotted, this miner looked less harmful, so I approached him.

"Young woman, you don't belong here," he said. "It's dangerous. You're from Brainsville, I suppose. Are you lost?"

"I was born here before all you miners came," I said. "I know this satellite well. Certainly better than any miner." That was a bit of snippy braggadocio, but it was a reaction more to the "are you lost?" question than the "don't belong here" and "it's dangerous" comments.

He shrugged. "But you don't know Middle Finger well. Come inside." I hesitated. "I'm not going to bite you, but I don't like my colleagues salivating over you either. It's creepy."

Because I agreed with that perception, I entered the tent. In spite of his slovenly, sweaty appearance, it looked clean and orderly. The front part looked like a store that had no inventory, just a long and dusty counter with some old equipment upon it. I thought I spotted electronic scales, a mass spectrometer, and an assortment of hand tools. I guessed a doorway with a canvas covering in back of the counter led into his personal quarters.

"My name's Asako Kobayashi. What's yours?"

"Daniel Chang." He offered his hand. I shook it. "Guess I'm the scientist here. I assay the ore." He pointed to a radiation suit hanging from a tent pole. "Some of it's radioactive, but don't worry, I won't glow in the dark. By assaying, I can warn the miners about that as well as tell them the value of what they've found."

"How do they pay you?"

He laughed. "We have a bartering system for the most part. They give me some of their rations or their drink in payment. Works for me. Want some ale? Our in-camp doctor makes it right here following a recipe of some Earth monks."

I knew about recipes now, but I doubted this one—I knew most monasteries in Earth's history guarded their brewing secrets. Besides, there weren't any left after the Tali invasion, but maybe there were computer records?

"I'd rather have some water, but I first need a place to pee."

"There's a tree in back of the tent." I shook my head. "Yeah, understood. Take this stool and lean forward. Best I can do." He gave me a folding stool with a canvas seat.

I walked out the front and around to the back of the tent where I did my business and then returned. A glass of cold water was waiting for me. It looked a bit cloudy, but it was wet and cleaner than the water in the Fistians' cistern.

***

"I'm going to write an exosociological thesis about Fistian culture," I said after gulping half the water. Even with shade and the light breeze in the tent, Hard Fist's climate was hard to take. I envied Daniel's minimal wardrobe, but no way was I going shirtless in the mining camp. And I wondered what he put on during the cold nights. Maybe he had a parka stashed in his quarters? The tent seemed drafty—good for the day temps, but bad for the night ones. "I need to include miners' viewpoints about them."

"I have no quarrel with them," said Daniel, "but most miners think they're stupid, filthy beasts, and a damn nuisance. One tried to sell us some vegetables. I thought that was a nice gesture and a chance to improve our diets, but the others didn't. They ran him right out of town."

Filthy beasts? I smiled at the irony. Thought maybe the miners' opinion implied they were the ones who were stupid, not Fistians.

"That's a bigoted attitude. Are there any particular justifications for that opinion?" I knew there weren't, but I wanted him to admit it.

He shook his head. "We don't mix with them. I think it's just the xenophobia of ignorant people. My colleagues are all self-absorbed and only care about the quality and price of the ore they mine. They don't even care much about their other colleagues, let alone local flora and fauna." He eyed me up and down—not exactly an ogle, but I felt uncomfortable. "How old are you?"

"Old enough. Why?"

"No criticism intended, but you might have grown up here and consequently have an incorrect and biased opinion about Fistians. You're not old enough to have a Human perspective, young lady."

"This is their planet."

"Probably not for long. The ore ships will have to increase in number to haul out what's been mined, and that will eventually mean a large spaceport, and then miners will start bringing their dyads and triads and children. Maybe even before that. Happens all the time on these frontier planets. The standard progression. I've lived through it many times."

"Because it's not regulated."

He nodded. "Can't be. Hard Fist isn't a member of ITUIP. The only possible regulators are miners, and they want fewer regulations, not more."

ITUIP had regulations that member planets had to abide by. Non-members like Hard Fist followed them only when convenient. In a place where small mining camps dominated, it never would be convenient. Daniel was right. It happened all the time, and not just with miners. Religious groups and other ranchers and farmers looking for a simpler life fled from crowded planets where they considered their way of life was persecuted. Sometimes it was, but it also often came down to not accepting other people's opinions, religions, or customs. That diaspora from ITUIP included ETs as well as Humans, but they were usually segregated among among the frontier planets.

"So you envision a bleak future for native Fistians?"

"Unless something happens to change miners' minds about them. I envision a bleak future here for Human scientists and engineers too. You best tell them they'll have to abandon Hard Fist soon."

"You're here because of what one of our exogeologists found," I said.

"That's true. Think the miners will care about that if you folks or Fistians get in their way? Especially Fistians. Of course, you're welcome to stay. A good-looking girl like you could make a lot of money from tips as a waitperson or hospitality girl in a bar. We can't afford server robots on a frontier world, and females are scarce in the mining camps."

My opinion about Daniel took a nosedive.

***

I looked back on the camp as I walked out of the tent town. A thick haze hung over it, a combination of dust and smoke and probably generic pollution from strip-mining operations. I wasn't planning on going back soon. Someone else could do a thesis about mining camps on Hard Fist if they wanted. I had enough information about their perception of the Fistians and didn't much care about any part of it.

Wondered how much of the planet's environment they'd already destroyed. *Will the miners undo the careful balance Fistians have created and want to maintain? Will Fistians strike back at Humans for letting the destruction of their environment occur?* My home had an uncertain future, and it wasn't looking good.

I stopped by Marcello's village on the way back to Brainsville. He met me ambling into town.

"I can tell you aren't happy," he said as I mounted him. "That bad, right?"

"The miners are about the worst Humans you can imagine," I said, gripping his mane. "Take me for a ride so I can forget about them."

"There will be more coming. Mama Dora says Humans will overrun the planet if they can…and we let them."

"There's a solution," I said. "You can join forces with Human scientists, and we can petition for admission to ITUIP."

We were already out of the village and moving through the forest. We reached a clearing and I dismounted. He sat on his butt and eyed me.

"Only three problems with your plan: Many of your scientists wouldn't even want that, the miners certainly won't, and many of us want nothing to do with some distant Human organization either. We were fine here before Humans arrived. Nothing against you, Asako, but not even Human scientists have accepted us. You're the first Human to visit our village and mingle with us in a friendly way."

I wanted to say, "Why didn't you ask?" *But why should they?* Except for Lars Swensen, who explored Fistian ruins, most scientists were only interested in Fistians as part of the fauna in Hard Fist's ecosystem, not as social equals. One of my goals was to change that.

"ITUIP isn't a Human organization. Other intelligent beings originating on many different planets are part of the Union. You should go and see what goes on in some ITUIP worlds. Aren't you interested?"

"Not me. OK, maybe a little, from the point of view of seeing new science and technology and more motivated by trying to help my people. But I'm not in charge. And each village is independent. We're friendly among ourselves, but independent."

"I know that. So are ITUIP worlds." I thought a moment and decided to change the topic a bit. "Your people have been here forever. Has it always been a society built around small villages?"

He hesitated. "We don't talk about those things," he finally said. "Look, I understand your frustration and can see we have a major Fistian-Human disconnect, but ITUIP is too remote. It can't be the solution to our problems."

I sighed. "I'll keep studying your people and hope that things don't get too bad too fast. Maybe we'll find a solution. I'm not optimistic."

Chapter Fifteen

I stayed in Marcello's village, feeling comfortable and safe there. Brainsville wasn't as xenophobic as the mining camps, but it was still nice to avoid stares and glares from scientists who at best thought I was wasting my time, and at worst were completely hostile to me or considered me a sexual object. You can't help but sense when people disapprove or undress you mentally. I wasn't sure all Fistians approved of my presence, but at least they never exhibited any outright antagonism.

"You're very busy," I said after my shower the next morning as I watched Marcello concentrate on some mathematical problem. "Shower" was a misnomer, of course; it consisted of pouring water over myself several times in a corner of one area of Marcello's small dwelling designed for that purpose. Because that area was designed for Marcello's size, I had plenty of room, just not plenty of water. "Am I distracting you?"

"Never." He eyed me as I toweled off. "Mama Dora says you should find a mate."

I blushed. *Does he know about Doc?* There was no way my parents told him. They wouldn't want any gossip among Humans, let alone Fistians. "If Mama Dora could conjure up an acceptable fellow from the Fistian mists, maybe I would." I'd have to call him Phoenix if the mists were the ones rising from the lava river at ocean's edge. I couldn't think of another appropriate mythological name for a lover conjured up from that or the rainforest steam after a thundershower.

"I don't know what that means. She's simply saying you've reached breeding age."

I frowned. "We Humans tend to delay that a bit now. We live a lot longer than we did during our home planet's primitive times. Mama Dora's giving too much importance to Human physiology and not enough to Human sociology."

"I can understand that statement a bit. I'm sorry for repeating Mama Dora's opinion, and I apologize. Maybe you should talk to her?"

I pulled on my jersey, pants, and boots. "No way! It's too hard to win arguments with Mama Dora."

"I'll agree with that." He indicated the large tablet computer's screen that I'd stolen from Brainsville supplies for him so he didn't have to scratch equations on tree bark or in the dirt, something I soon selfishly regretted because he now spent more time with the tablet than with me. "I've discovered an anomaly in our orbit."

"Let me see." I moved forward to study the equations. "I'm not very good at deciphering anyone's equations, not even mine." It didn't help that Fistian writing used ideograms. The equations became hard to decipher when there were many ideograms because they all looked similar to the untrained eye. "Can you make a diagram of what you found?"

"Better than that, I can plot the orbit," he said. "The software on this little machine is very good."

Didn't want to tell him the software was more Brainsville's AI's doing—that little machine wasn't much more than graphical display equipment, and any calculations were something I could do with my wi-fi implant if I could communicate with the AI. After some clicks and vocal commands, the screen cleared. I saw something akin to ellipses, the sharp ends in precession around one of the focii.

"At one focal point is Big Fellow. The planet's so big that its gravity dominates, of course. Hard Fist's orbit isn't just one ellipse like we always thought it was. This new orbital plot matches data I've puzzled over for a while. I needed to add an arbitrary term to the dynamical equations to match the data."

I smiled. *The scientific method at work!* I understood data driving theory. Although I didn't completely understand what he'd done, I wanted him to continue. "Have you allowed for perturbations from Big Fellow's other moons?"

"I've estimated their effect. They'd be there in a complete multibody approximation, but they aren't big enough to produce that extra term."

"So what could cause it?"

"Can you ask your AI?"

I was reluctant to do that. I'd always appreciated the aha!-moments in my life—my epiphany on that ledge long ago came to mind—so I didn't want to deprive Marcello of that same pleasure. But my own curiosity beat me into submission.

The little tablet computer was connected via an RF-link I'd cobbled together to Brainsville's computing complex managed by the scientists' irascible AI Einstein. If the wi-fi device had more power, I could do the same thing with that. I was rather proud of the setup. My electronic skills weren't that great.

"I could, but I'm not sure what to ask it." I sat down in front of the screen. "As a start, let me just ask Einstein if it recognizes your equation. It can do that in a blink of an eye."

Not quite. While Einstein pondered Marcello's equation—I'm sure the ideographs were holding it up too—we went to Mama Dora's for breakfast.

"No talk about mating," I said to Marcello in a whisper as we entered.

"Of course not," he said. "Mama Dora doesn't have to know everything."

Mama Dora had several elders from other clans as guests for breakfast that morning, which is why she'd invited us to observe. They were very polite and made room for Marcello and me in their circle. I was both pleased and humbled and saw an opportunity.

"Do your people have some kind of worldwide organization?" I said when there was a pause in their conversation. I dipped my fingers into the water bowl so I could scoop out another handful of mush from the big communal pot. "I haven't observed one."

Drel, a wizened Fistian male about twice Marcello's size and even larger than Mama Dora, whom he resembled, was the first to answer. He stood, bowed, and beat off a few flies with his tail while pacing a bit before answering. It made me think of pontificating Human professors on Sanctuary pacing on the stage as they lectured. I recalled that Denise Amalfi had hated that, but I always wrote it off as either nerves or an aid to thinking, figuring I'd probably do it myself in that situation—and probably make a worse lecture while doing so.

The visiting elders were a mixed group. Some were clan mothers too, like Mama Dora; those were smaller females with pelts of different colors. Others were males who showed deference to the elderly females. A few knew Standard, and those few translated for the others when it was necessary. I was happy to be at that meeting and hoped I could remember everything about it—they wouldn't have understood a need for taking notes because Fistian memories were prodigious and most likely eidetic.

Drel was just one of the gang but seemed chummier with Mama Dora. I learned later that he was her father. That explained the resemblance. Contrary to what other Humans on Hard Fist thought, not all Fistians look alike. If you are around them long enough, you can easily see differences.

Drel knew Standard and gave me an official welcome.

"Welcome to our gathering, First Born among Humans on Hard Fist. We've heard about you in our other villages, which leads in nicely to my attempting to provide an answer to your question. It depends on what you mean by worldwide organization. From what I've learned about you Humans, you seem to need that more than we do. Our ancestors suggest to us what is right and wrong, for example, so we don't need a rigid set of rules or authority to enforce them. The occasional criminal is simply banished from all the villages and must survive anyway she or he can." He dropped his head; I knew that meant sorrow or anguish. "That's usually a death sentence, of course. Hard Fist can be unforgiving when Fistians violate her wishes."

Oh great. Did I miss pantheism? That could explain the tender loving care the Fistians gave to the environment. *Were their gods among the flora and fauna of the satellite?*

"What about building new villages? I know you just do that when one becomes too large, but who decides where to build?"

"Those who will settle in the new village select a location and, if the ancestors agree, all discussion ends.

That process isn't very complicated, but it always has to be done with respect for the planet. We only borrow the land, air, water, and sky and return it all to the planet when we pass on."

I was getting a bit frustrated. "So these ancestors are a governing group somewhere that makes all the important decisions?"

"Yes, a large group, but no decisions. Only suggestions and opinions. We generally follow them, but there are a few exceptions. For the location of a village, for example, sometimes the course of a river has changed. They can't know about such things. It would not be appropriate to construct a new village in the middle of a raging river, would it?"

"I think that's enough Fistian culture for Asako," said Mama Dora. "You will talk the Human child to death, and she won't get enough nourishment by listening to you prattle on. Let her enjoy her breakfast."

I added some spices to the glop in my right hand with my left. That made it more exciting to eat. I knew the glop was nutritious, but the pasty substance became boring with time without spices. Of course, any food can become boring if you eat it all the time, but the variety of natural spices Mama Dora offered helped alleviate the boredom.

I spent the remainder of the time eating and listening. I was starting to pick up some Fistian words. The best way to learn a language is to listen and try to speak it as much as possible. I just wished I could pick up Fistian as easily as they picked up Standard.

***

"I'd like to learn more about these ancestors," I said, entering Marcello's smaller dwelling again after returning from breakfast.

"I think we have an answer!" he said.

I saw the blinking green light on his computer. Typical male, thinking what he was doing was more important than what I was doing. *Will I ever get my thesis written?*

The memory of our only disagreement reared its ugly head. *Is Marcello's realization of his dreams becoming a barrier to realizing mine?* I soon rejected that notion for a more positive one: *if I help Marcello realize his dreams, maybe he'll be more motivated to help me realize mine.*

"I'm not sure I understand Einstein's answer, though."

Marcello had brought up the text message from the AI instead of the voice message. Einstein randomly chose different voices; some strident and irritating even for me as well as whispery and hardly intelligible, but Fistians have more sensitive ears they can orient to catch soundwaves better. Marcello still tended not to trust his understanding of spoken Standard, although he was very good at reading and speaking it.

I read through the message. It had links to several scientific documents in the form of computer files. One was in German; the author was Einstein's namesake. *Of course!*

"I think you've stumbled upon the cubic term needed to approximately describe the orbital motion of any small body in orbit around a much more massive one. Back in Earth's history, they observed that the one-over-r term in the potential couldn't account for the complete motion of the planet Mercury around Earth's sun." I didn't know German; I was just remembering some science history. "Big Fellow is almost a star, and Hard Fist is its closest satellite. It's a comparable problem. I'm surprised your astronomers could detect the much tinier deviations, though, especially with the tiny perturbations caused by other satellites."

"We take simultaneous measurements from multiple sites," said Marcello, "and we've done that for a while. Your AI has helped me organize that data. So, am I on to something?"

Are they performing interferometry? And what does "we" mean? Is Marcello communicating with scientists around Hard Fist?

I couldn't explain General Relativity to Marcello because I didn't even understand its rudiments myself. And I would go completely insane trying to explain how struggles to reconcile that theory with quantum mechanics eventually, but in a roundabout way, led to our FTL interstellar drives.

I told him to strike up a conversation with Einstein the AI, knowing Human scientists had programmed in some failsafe mechanisms that would make that conversation more Socratic—in other words, lead Marcello to discover the answers to his own queries.

But his comments started me down my own path of inquiry that could be important for my thesis. Somehow Fistians maintained a collective knowledge over time— "we've done it for a while" he'd said about the data. *The ancestors? And is science the foundation for the Fistians' social organization?* I needed answers to those questions. I could imagine Lonely Swimmer and other members of my thesis committee chastising me if I didn't have them.

Chapter Sixteen

I felt honored when Drel invited me to his village. Located on a large island just off the coast from Mama Dora's and Brainsville, it offered me a chance to observe Fistian life in a different village other than the one I knew so well. I had to broaden my research vistas—just one village doesn't make a good statistical sample. That flight with my father didn't count as close scientific observations of Fistian culture either.

It was my first trip in a Fistian boat. I'd never been on a boat before, Fistian, Human, or otherwise. I knew the principles. You had to build something that floats, although that's easier in salt water than fresh water. You need some kind of locomotion—boats use either wind, motors, or muscles. This Fistian boat was more flat and looked less safe than those I'd seen in pictures of Human boats—a large, flat raft with half-meter sides to keep water out, and it had a center pole for a sail as well as oars and a rudder. Nothing fancy, to be sure.

Drel used the oars to get us past the reef and then raised sail.

"Want to steer?" he said.

I looked at the large rudder, built for Fistian muscles, and wondered if I'd have the strength. "I've never done that," I said.

"Nothing to it," he said. He gave me a brief lesson. "Just keep the boat pointed to that area on the island's coast."

He sat down on his haunches and started to sing. His songs were ethereal and soothing, and I would have dozed off if I hadn't been concentrated on keeping the boat on course. Maybe that was Drel's plan? Or, did he just want to sing?

"Are boats like this one the main vehicles used to go from continent to continent and island to island?" I said when one song ended.

"We have no other transportation now," he said, "and we'd like to keep it that way. Hard Fist has provided us with food from its waters too, as you've probably seen on market day. Land, air, and sea—who can ask for anything more?"

I focused on that word "now." *What does that mean? Did they have other means before? If so, how long ago?* I asked him.

"We don't focus on the past, Asako," he said, and went back to his singing.

***

Our voyage wasn't over when we made landfall. Drell had me climb on his back, a bit harder to do than it was with Marcello, and we headed inland.

His island was even lusher than the area around Mama Dora's village. And warmer. I decided I had too many clothes on. *Will I insult him if I strip down?* I decided not to chance it. Fistians wear no clothing other than some occasional ornamental things, but I thought I might shock him if he wasn't used to seeing naked Humans. Marcello never seemed to care, but he was a liberal Fistian for the most part. *Except for those damned ancestors!* Fistians mentioned them a lot, belying what Drel said— they do focus on the past! And they seem to make decisions based on some kind of communication with them. I wondered if they got high on some natural psychedelic.

The blister vines and large insects were ubiquitous on the island too—maybe even more so. "Does this island have any droolers?" I was hoping he'd say no. I was rewarded.

"It used too. They died out here. They'd have nothing much to eat now except us, and we don't particularly want to make the personal sacrifice to feed them."

I could see his dancing eyebrows even from my perch atop him, so I knew that was a joke.

"Is your village newer or older than Mama Dora's?"

"Older. Dora left here when we decided to create her village. That is our custom. We have spread across Hard Fist doing just that."

"I know. I saw villages from the air. But why are they so small. If you find a suitable place, why doesn't the population just increase there?"

"We have learned not to do that."

Learned? Did they do it before? I asked him that in a roundabout fashion.

"We look toward the future now, not the past. Watch that branch!"

I ducked just in time when a branch he'd pushed aside came swinging towards me. I wondered if he'd done it on purpose or as a warning. *Do my questions annoy him?*

"Am I asking too many questions?"

"You have the curiosity of the young. Even our young must be taught to temper curiosity with respect for Hard Fist, its people, and our ancestors."

***

We were halfway to Drel's village when a storm turned the sky dark. Hard Fist had all kinds of storms, of course, from gentle rains to storms with winds of a hundred knots or more that could flatten many acres of rainforest. They all implied torrents of water falling from the sky. They were a bit more tolerable in the day than during the cold nights.

Drel and I found shelter beneath a rock ledge.

"This storm blew in from the open ocean. We could be in danger."

I was drenched. Even in the steamy heat, my teeth chattered, because it was a bit like nightfall with the sun gone. "Will it turn to snow or sleet?"

Drell thought a moment. Perhaps he was puzzling over Standard's different words for frozen precip. I'd never seen either form. There hadn't been any chance to do that on Sanctuary.

"Probably not. The atmosphere is superheated above the storm. They usually occur when that condition combines with a new volcanic eruption on some far-away island." He paused as we watched three trees fall, take off, and fly away like rocket sleds. "Once the eye passes ua, the wind will change direction. We could be in trouble then."

"Will your village be in danger?"

"Probably not. These storms tend to be localized and move fast. At Dora's village, they'd never see anything this bad either, although the remnants of this one might get there. The winds tend to lose energy at higher elevations. From space you'd see more of the eye's movement as if it were dragging a huge cloud along the storm's path."

Space? Had Drel been in space? "How big is the storm?"

Drel thought a moment. "Anywhere from twenty to fifty kilometers in diameter. Let's hope this one is at the lower end of that range."

Suddenly there was silence, the bright sun reappeared in a clear sky, and the rainforest looked almost normal. It didn't sound normal, though. You become used to its sounds, and their absence was eerie.

The rainforest fauna had known what was coming. Within a short time, the winds were back. We were also bombarded by many of those huge insects; they were either dead or dying. We were soon covered by insect innards and surrounded by their carcasses.

I stood so the rain would rinse me off. Drel pulled me down.

"It's better to keep a low profile. You never know what the winds will bring. And sometimes there's lightning. We'll wash off after the storm passes."

Drel knew where to do that, of course. We both felt better after we got rid of the goo.

***

Drel's village was almost a carbon copy of Mama Dora's. I met his clan mother, a Fistian who looked even more ancient than Dora. We arrived just before the midday nap. I wandered around the village while they were all resting.

While the layout was similar, this village seemed a bit larger and had a lot more constructions that provided shade because it was warmer on the island. And not only constructions; they took a lot more advantage of natural shade from trees. I saw fewer cultivated fields, though, but maybe water was less plentiful because the village's river was smaller?

Most villagers didn't know Standard. The clan mother and Drel had to serve as interpreters. I suspected that in even more remote villages, I wouldn't be able to communicate at all.

But these villagers were festive too. A big celebration started up toward evening. It seemed a lot more boisterous than the market day celebrations in Marcello's village.

"Is something special going on today? Is it some kind of holiday?"

Drel's eyebrows danced. "Something like that. You are about to witness a wedding. There's celebration before, during, and after. Here come the bride and groom now."

The Fistian bride galloped into the circle of revelers and bowed to everyone. She had wildflowers woven into her mane and carried a blanket of them on her back. She remained bowing when she came to the clan mother. The groom then entered more sedately, bowed to everyone, and then remained by the bride. When the clan mother stood up, they both rose and stood before her.

"I'll translate for you," said Drel in a whisper. "'Mizo and Jacko, do you come before me to ask for my permission to wed?' The bride and groom now say, 'We do!' Now the clan mother says, 'Does anyone object to this union?' When no one does, she will say, 'The permission is given.'"

I watched the bride and groom trot off while everyone stood and cheered.

"That's it?" I said to Drel.

"They've had a long courtship. No one would object."

"I meant that it seems that the ceremony is so simple."

"There's nothing more to say. We don't belabor the point. Life must go on."

"And where are the parents?"

Drel's eyebrows danced again. "I'm the proud father of the bride. Another one of my daughters has become someone else's problem! They were waiting for me to have the ceremony. I imagine she was very impatient."

"And probably hating me because of it."

"No. Both bride and groom felt honored by your presence. Besides, everyone on Hard Fist knows you want to study us. How could your study ever be complete without experiencing a ceremony like this one? Come, Asako, and partake of food and drink. The celebration will continue until tomorrow morning, but it's better to join in earlier when all the food is still fresh and the drinks are plentiful."

I stored one observation away for my thesis. Like primitive Humans, the Fistians didn't have anything like triads or dyads of the same sex. They didn't even have triads. I would have to complement that observation, though. First, did they consider that unusual among Humans? Second, did any Fistians have such inclinations, but the others didn't allow those kind of relationships? Those were perhaps indiscreet questions, so I decided to save them for Marcello where I had more confidence that I wouldn't make him feel uncomfortable.

But as I was walking toward the line forming around the huge pots, I was thinking that I'd like to have a wedding ceremony like that—simple and to the point. Maybe Mama Dora could perform it! But maybe she wouldn't if it were a triad?

I decided then that being an exosociologist could get me into trouble I normally wouldn't have.

Chapter Seventeen

The next day Drel invited me to go fishing. I had no idea what that meant exactly, so I said yes.

We returned to the coast but on the other side of the island facing the open ocean where there were a large number of boats. Drel introduced me to the whole group of Fistians waiting there, and we climbed aboard one raft where a young Fistian male was already onboard.

None of the Fistians spoke Standard except for Drel, so on our raft he served as translator again. Soon we far enough out that we'd lost sight of the island.

They all seemed excited when we found an area of quiet water covered by some oily substance that had damped the ocean waves. The Fistians started chanting. I about lost my breakfast when a huge animal breached the surface not more than five meters away from our boat.

The young Fistians stood in their rafts and tossed spears with ropes attached. All of us then went for a ride as the beast pulled us along.

I felt sorry for the creature, but I recognized it represented a protein supplement to the Fistian diet. When it finally expired, a few rafts pulled it close, and the whole fleet headed home.

***

Back on shore, the animal was drawn up on the crude docks. It had a large head with a long snout and feet that looked like oars. There seemed to be a thin coat of fur all over it.

"It doesn't look so big here on land," I said to Drel.

"But Hard Fist has made it strong. Our hunting culls the weak and the old, so the remainder can become stronger. It is the way of the ancestors."

Something else to note for the thesis. The Fistians were predators, but they were careful about how they went about doing it.

"These provide the slabs of meat in the markets?"

"In my village, yes; in Mama Dora's, only occasionally. They have more land animals around there to provide nourishment."

"And what's this beast called?"

My breakfast was still in danger as I glanced at the butchering operation. Drell pronounced a Fistian word. I repeated it.

"Very good, Asako. You have a knack for languages."

"Not old Mandarin or English," I said.

"Perhaps you have less motivation to learn those."

Wise old Fistian! "Females aren't allowed on these hunting trips?"

"Sometimes. When we go after bigger game, especially. There are many creatures in our oceans. Dora could throw a mean spear in her youth."

I'd seen how the young Fistians had tossed those spears with their long arms. It reminded me of when I played with a slingshot as a girl, only they had Fistian muscles, not those of a little Human waif.

"And what's the reason for the singing?"

"We are calling the beasts from the depths. The bigger the slick is, the older the beast. We use that to cull only the old and the weak."

***

The young Fistians wrapped all the meat in wet leaves and tied bundles of it on their backs. We then headed back to Drel's village at a leisurely pace.

"What will you do with all the meat?" I said to Drel as I held tightly onto his mane.

"Some will be consumed now, but most will be salted and dried for later use. The fattier pieces will be used in cooking."

"Hard Fist provides," I said.

"You're getting the idea," said Drel.

"I've learned a lot these last two days. Thanks for inviting me."

"You are most welcome, First Born. Our lives here are hard, but they're also simple."

"Complex enough," I said. "I'm very sorry no other Human has tried to learn more about your culture here on Hard Fist."

"There always has to be a first."

Is that a compliment? I was starting to think the old guy liked me. Marcello, Mama Dora, and Drel—I now felt very close to three Fistians. And I liked all of them.

Chapter Eighteen

After we returned to Mama Dora's village, I had to go home to change clothes. My parents let me go about my business those days without much supervision (it had always been annoying but never oppressive), so I was surprised when my angry father entered and slammed the door. *Is he mad because I stayed overnight with Fistian folk? Why do I have to ask his permission?*

"Anything wrong?" I said, trying to look innocent. I was eating some sugar cookies and drinking some of the sappy liquid they still called milk—powdered stuff you added water to. Fistian food was nutritional but boring, and I needed a sugar fix. "You're never here so early in the afternoon."

"I'm calling a meeting of the Science Council. The miners are out of control."

I studied Dad2 for a moment. He was a short, muscular man with a chiseled face, black hair and eyes, and a very gentle person for all his intensity. His one trait that endeared him to me was respect for everyone. That often seemed to be out of synch with his indifference toward Fistians, but maybe things were changing?

OK, he's not mad at me. Worse. He's indifferent to me. He probably didn't even know I was gone!

"Haven't they always been?" I said.

"Yeah, but they kept to themselves for the most part, so we ignored them and considered their actions as just the result of adapting to a new and strange place. They arrived soon after you left. But now we've discovered some new deposits upriver from the Fistian village. If

117

they mine them, all their waste products from the mining operations will wash downriver."

"We have to stop them! Some of those rare earths are radioactive and others are toxic and will poison the river."

"I know. But I don't know how to stop them."

"And you think the Council does?"

He plopped into the chair opposite me with a sigh. I'd never seen him so frustrated.

"Probably not. And without ITUIP to come down on the miners, they'll probably get away with it."

"I can organize the Fistians. We'll protest and stand up to them."

"That can backfire, Asako. You don't know the miners. They're lowlife thugs who have come here from many worlds to seek their fortunes. I don't think they care about us, let alone Fistians."

Strong words from Dad2. No scientist, not even him, could be called a Fistian fan. Feelings ran the gamut from being annoyed that Fistians got in the way of their research to open hostility toward Marcello's people. My parents had generally been in the first group but had improved as I became more involved with Marcello as a kid and Fistians in general later. Maybe I should have told them Marcello had saved my life.

As a kid? I smiled. It was just a short time ago. To my father maybe I was still his kid; certainly to me he was still Dad2. It sounded like this apolitical Human was on the right side of a Hard Fist issue this time.

"Do you think the miners will become violent if we protest?" I said.

He nodded. I decided I didn't care. There were principles involved, the biggest one being that Fistians were on Hard Fist first—the planet was theirs, not ours!

"We can't fight the miners," Lars Swensen said as the chairperson of the Science Council. That set the scientists at the meeting off again. He shook his head and gaveled them into silence. "One at a time, damn it!"

Lars was the oldest scientist at Brainsville. He was an exoarchaeologist who mostly studied Fistian ruins, but he'd been instrumental in deciphering some of their writing too, with the help of Einstein, of course. He was also the biggest Human I knew and very strong, but he was gentle too, like Dad2. Sort of like Marcello in a way. Or Mama Dora or Drel. Of all the scientists, he probably understood me best, even better than Mom or Dad2.

Lars was like a second father, in fact, maybe because he'd lost his best friend, Dad1, who had been an electronic tech and got fried by a short in a power hookup just after the scientific mission had landed and began its work on Hard Fist. I was born into a dyad instead of a triad for that reason. Dad1 and Dad 2 looked enough alike that stirring Mom's genes into the pot and fixing a few errors left me looking a bit like all three and no one in particular, but still not knowing who my real biological father was. My surname was Kobayashi only because Dad2 was the oldest member of the triad—that was a naming convention but not a hard-and-fast rule.

Dad1 had known computers inside and out. He had set up our AI Einstein and hacked into the Hard Fist expedition's DNA records (considered private) to look at the triad's genetic background. He discovered Mom could trace her bloodline all the way back to the first permanent scientific station on Dione, one of Saturn's moons; Dad1 to the first Chinese colonists on Mars; and Dad2 to Peru long before Humans even visited Earth's moon. In theory, I could figure out who my biological father was by also using those DNA records, but I had never done that. Lars, in some sense, had become a substitute for Dad1.

All that history flooded into my crazy head as Lars pointed to a tall woman three rows in front of me. Like my father, Karen McCarthy was an exogeologist. She had discovered the rare earth deposits on the planet, including the ones above Marcello's village. I wondered if she regretted that now.

She was a slender, nervous woman with angular features and more pronounced epicanthic folds than Dad2's. She also tended to slouch in chairs because of her height. She wore a bikini top and shorts most of the time, showing off long, sexy legs, but she ruined the effect by wearing hiking boots that would have made my feet swell in the oppressive heat.

She was known for speaking her mind. On second thought, I figured she neither regretted nor celebrated finding the rare earth deposits. She would just consider it part of her job and had stopped thinking about it.

I didn't know if she liked Fistians or not, but her next words suggested she was on the side of fairness.

"I just want to point out that we should warn the Fistians. Not to do so would lump us together with the miners, maybe to our detriment. That doesn't appeal to me personally."

"The miners are just a bunch of violent and greedy Humans," I said in a low voice.

"What's that, Asako?" said Lars.

"Never mind. Karen's right. The least you can do is inform the Fistians. If you're incapable of doing that, I will."

"You've always loved those smelly centaurs more than your own kind," Sam Rivers said with a growl. "Why don't you go back to their village and stay there? We know which side you're on!"

Where Lars was gentle, Sam was as rough as a blister vine. He swore a lot. Mom said he could have been a miner because he was so uncouth. I wasn't naïve enough to think all miners were bad. And I was mature enough to realize that the most vocal and ready to protest among scientists and miners were often in the minority. Most of the remainder were indifferent, which was a big problem.

Sam was certainly vocal. As a big man, he tended to bellow like the Fistians he despised, but he wasn't laughing most of the time, except his bellows weren't laughter. Mom called him a sourpuss. He got after me as a child once when I snuck into his chemistry lab and started playing with chemicals and equipment. I might have wasted some chemicals, and maybe he was just looking out for my safety. Mom suggested the latter, and banned me from going near the place. Later on, though, he had shown me how to mix up some awful smelling stuff that mimicked the stench of the pond Marcello had dunked me in. Payback was only partial—I got some of the smelly gook on me too. That was enough to show me that old Sam had at least two sides to his behavioral patterns.

Most people do, of course—many sides, actually. In a way, I had developed an understanding of Humans a lot slower than I'd done with my understanding of Fistians. But I knew enough to avoid pushing buttons that would anger the people in Brainsville. Fistians represented a Sam-button that I wasn't going to avoid this time, though. I readied myself for more verbal battle.

Sam's outburst set them off again. Lars brought the meeting to order.

"Those kind of comments shouldn't come from a scientist," said Lars. He nodded at me. "As the leading expert on native Fistian culture, do you think they'll attack us or the miners?"

"If we tell them we're not in favor of what the miners plan," I said, calming down and mentally thanking Lars, "I don't think they will attack Brainsville. I don't know about the miners. The Fistians won't be keen on moving their village, no matter what, so they'll at least protest. I plan to join them on that."

"Typical attitude from a brat who's full of herself," said Sam. "What's your father say? Would you go against his wishes?"

I looked at Dad2. He was studying the toes of his boots. I felt sorry for him. He must be between a rock and a hard place. I'd come across that expression once in a school reading assignment and liked it. It describes a situation where choices seem to be difficult. In his case, he might only be making them seem that way, but his silence was disturbing.

"Where's the nearest ITUIP ship?" said Karen, changing the subject.

"There might be some SEB ships nearby," said my mother, "but the nearest ITUIP planet is twenty-seven light-years away. I'm also not sure that ITUIP would want to get involved in something like this."

The ITUIP Space Exploration Bureau's ships represented the only contact we had with more civilized planets. Hard Fist was a pioneer world. But not for native Fistians!

"I move we adjourn and proceed to query them about this situation," said Sam. "It will be beneficial to keep on their good side in case we have to abandon the planet. Asako and her friends might soon be hunting us down!"

I left then but heard Lars start the vote on Sam's motion. I was sure they'd vote yes. They were incapable of doing anything constructive, so they'd delay the hard decisions and hand off the problem to someone else. Unfortunately that person seemed to be me.

***

Lars and I went to talk to the Fistians. I'd been wrong. I wasn't the first Human to visit the village. He was there before I was born to ask for permission to visit some of their ruins. He was that kind of guy, but that told me the ruins themselves weren't sacred. *But where else could the ancestors be?*

We sat with Mama Dora and a few local elders. Marcello stood in the back out of the way. I could tell he was puzzled and wondering what was happening.

Unlike the scientists in Brainsville, the Fistians took it calmly.

"We will not allow this," Mama Dora said in her simple fashion. "When they come upriver, we will stop them. Be assured of that, Human Scientist Swensen."

Lars nodded. "I was afraid you'd say that. The miners will be armed, you know."

"Do you think your puny weapons will scare us?" said one elder.

"They should," said Lars. "They scare me. And these fellows can be violent as hell. I hear fistfights in Middle Finger are a daily occurrence."

"I'm not familiar with this Human concept of hell," said Mama Dora. "But Asako and I have discussed Humans and their history from when they were planet-bound to the present. It is a history of great deeds mixed with violent upheavals. For now, let's assume the miners will be reasonable. There are other deposits they can

123

mine. They want those near our village only out of convenience."

I nodded. There was a lot of truth to that. Maybe Fistians were interested in mining during their long history, but they didn't seem to have any interest in doing so now. They didn't seem to care about ore deposits at all.

"I don't suppose you could move the village to somewhere above the deposits," said Lars.

"Out of the question," said Mother Dora. "Our ancestors would never permit it."

Lars looked at me. I shrugged. Here I was the leading expert on Fistian culture and I still couldn't figure out who these damn ancestors were.

"I take that to mean that these grounds are sacred in some way?" said Lars.

"Yes, in our way. We wanted to build here because it's where the ground, the sky, and the waters meet in friendly embrace, and the ancestors concurred."

"I'll pass that along to the scientists in Brainsville. When ITUIP intercedes, it will be a good argument on your behalf." Lars struggled up from his lotus position and bowed to Mama Dora and the other elders. "My business here is done. Thank you for listening. Coming, Asako?"

"I want to stay and talk to Marcello."

"See you back in Brainsville then."

"That was interesting," Marcello said after the meeting broke up. "I'm guessing you made your scientists tell us about the miners' plans?"

"I didn't have to do that. They voted to do so. They're not bad people for the most part. They know the miners can exploit other areas, so they don't want to cause Fistians any problems."

"It's peculiar that groups of Humans are often at odds."

"It's more peculiar that some groups of Humans let greed brainwash common sense right out of their minds," I said. "Take me for a ride and let's find a quiet place to talk."

A.B. CAROLAN

PART IV:
WAR CRIES

Chapter Nineteen

Daniel Chang later told me about the following events....

Boris Macar barged into Daniel's tent and grabbed him by his sweaty shoulders. "She's gone!"

Chang shook the miner off. "Settle down, will you? Who's gone?"

Boris was tugging at his beard and shaking his head. His eyes were wild. "Natasha, my daughter! She's been here only a week, and something's happened to her. I bet those damn Fistians are responsible."

The veins were bulging on his sweaty forehead. His bicep muscles, in arms as big around as Daniel's thighs, were twitching. Dad2 had once explained to me what Sumo wrestlers were. I'd researched them a bit more with Einstein. From Daniel's description, I guessed Boris looked like a raging Sumo wrestler who'd drunk too much sake. There are bad drunks and ones who just sleep it off. I imagined Boris was in the first set.

"Calm down. Did you leave her alone?"

"Of course. No one would hurt her here in Middle Finger. They know I'd kill'em!"

"Outside the mining towns, there's plenty on Hard Fist that's dangerous. But let's be optimistic: she probably went exploring and got lost."

"I'm rounding up some fellows and heading for that village," said Boris. "I see you won't be offering any help. You became friends with that scientist-brat Asako, right? She's probably helping Fistians create a strategy to put a stop to our digging plans, and this is what they came up with as a first step: kidnapping my daughter or worse.

Those scientists should never have told those stinking creatures about our plans."

"You're just jumping to conclusions all over the place today. Let me get you some water."

"Don't need water and I don't need more liquor, but if anything happens to my little girl, I sure will. And lots of Fistian blood." Boris stomped out of Chang's tent.

"Just what we need," Daniel said to himself, sitting down at his radio to call Brainsville and tell them about the mob of miners that might be heading for the Fistian village.

∗∗∗

There couldn't be two men more different than Boris Macar and Daniel Chang. I learned their hard-luck stories much later, but here's what I learned in summary…

Macar had lived his whole life by his brawn and not his brains. He had the latter knocked out of him as a bare-knuckles champion on the colony planet where he was born. He had found someone stupid enough to marry him among his many female admirers; they had a kid. He turned out to be a loving husband and father, something that didn't quite square with his xenophobia and brutish stubbornness. But who can make sense out of the contradictions existing in Human minds?

He now made his living mining, and that involved a lot of travelling from star system to star system working in mines on planets and asteroids where exogeologists like Dad2 had discovered rich lodes of rare earth metals needed elsewhere. I felt sorry for him in a way because that life had its ups and downs—he was a rich man at times and poor at others, the latter exacerbated by an addiction to gambling and drink that he fought to control.

Macar was a grim reminder of the lot of many people, Humans or ETs, who just muddled along through life without lofty goals or motivations beyond what was necessary to survive. These are often hearty and rugged people who resent interference in their lives and the intelligent lifeforms that cause it. They can do good and they can do evil, and I suppose it averages out in the long run.

Chang, on the other hand, was an introverted and quiet man. He was also a sporadic nomad who followed the path of discovery of new mining opportunities. He went with the flow and could make a living performing ore assays for miners—not a good living, but a comfortable one in the most primitive of mining outposts in near-Earth space, simply because he was the only one who did what he did.

He'd almost been an exogeologist but left school when a girlfriend jilted him. He was thoughtful and reasonable and often played the *de facto* mayor in mining communities for that reason, whether officially elected or not. A general medical doctor and someone like Chang were absolutely essential to those communities, and both were often paid via an old-fashioned barter system.

He needed funds to purchase equipment and supplies for his job, of course, and that need was the biggest complication in his life. It was usually satisfied by trading goods for money with crewmembers from the ore ships that regularly visited mining camps.

He was the closest person to a scientist, other than medical personnel, one could find among the miners. That didn't imply all his kind were good people because miners often set bad behavioral examples. Almost all mining communities now live on the frontiers of civilization and tend to ignore what goes on in the rest of near-Earth space.

I recognized that mining communities were necessary. Even though they were living on rugged frontiers, they formed one of many solid support groups for the advanced technologies that characterized the worlds of ITUIP.

***

I embellished a bit on Chang's story about the encounter with Macar, but that's the essence of what he told Dad2 over the radio. When the assayer signed off, I was out the door before my father could stop me. I ran to Marcello's village.

I found Mama Dora first and gave her a synopsis. "Thank you for the warning." She thought a moment. "This is maybe a good thing. The miners will see that we can defend ourselves. Leave that to me, First Born. Find Marcello and go look for that girl. I think Chang is right. She's new to the planet and probably wandered off to explore. Not knowing her way around, she could be lost and in trouble."

"Maybe in a drooler's belly," I said with a long face, knowing a seven-year-old can't run as fast as a thirteen-year-old. "Where's Marcello?"

"With his computer, where else? He's always calculating or modeling something these days since you gave him that tablet. He would have been a famous scientist in the old days."

"We have to talk about the ancestors and those old days," I said.

"That's not possible. Go find Marcello."

Not possible meaning never possible, or just not possible at the moment? I had to push that more, but I knew my priorities. I mounted Marcello after I found him, and we galloped toward Middle Finger, figuring the girl was probably somewhere between there and the village.

She wasn't. We had to expand our search area.

Fistians are more hunters and trackers than they are farmers. Like Humans, they're omnivores, but they aren't herders. The meat that went into their stewpots or they dried and salted was wild—either from the rainforests or the ocean, and, as they put it, borrowed from the planet to provide protein for their people. Tracking was an integral part of the hunts on land. Marcello came up with a search plan as if he were hunting the little girl.

***

I learned later that my father called an emergency meeting of the Council. They voted to also send out teams to look for the girl. Like two Caribbean pirate ships fighting over the same booty (were those stories real?), the team led by Sam Rivers met the team led by Boris Macar. Sam was more reasonable than Boris, and maybe cutting the miner some slack because he was worried about his little girl.

"You brilliant fellows out here to celebrate my daughter's death?" said Boris.

"We're trying to help find her, you idiot. That's an unfair accusation! Where have you looked already?"

That was a reasonable request. Sam didn't want to duplicate the other team's search efforts. Boris ignored the question.

"What's unfair is you telling those furry mutant horses about our mining plans. Now my daughter's dead or dying because some Fistians took their revenge."

"That's absurd! Fistians would never hurt your little girl. You're not thinking straight, man!"

Boris pushed Sam aside, almost knocking him to the ground. "Out of my way, genius. Go about your business. After I find my little darling, we're going to burn that village to the ground. And then attack Brainsville!"

"And you expect Fistians and scientists just to stand aside and let you do that?"

"You guys are worthless, arrogant bastards. They're brainless, stinking savages. Two incompetent extremes. What can you or they do to prevent it?"

"A lot, from our perspective. Unknown from the Fistians', but I'd be careful. They've never been afraid of us, I'll give them that. You might receive a rude awakening."

Boris nodded to his companions. "Here you have another centaur-lover. Let's get out of here."

But they gave up their search when they found the dead drooler and Natasha's red jersey.

Chapter Twenty

I couldn't have found the little girl without Marcello. We started searching along arcs with increasing radii and centered on the mining camp. An hour later he picked up a Human's scent, but there was also the powerful scent of an adult drooler whose stench even I could smell.

"This one is a big fellow," said Marcello, "and he's tracking the little Human. I don't think she knows. She seems lost and wandering."

"There!" I said, catching the glimpse of a red jersey high in a treetop.

"I see her. She's climbed the tree to escape, but the drooler is shaking the tree. I'll draw him away while you get the girl down."

I could see the red in the treetop swaying back and forth as the big drooler, standing on its hind legs, pounded the tree trunk with its front ones. *Maybe they aren't so dumb? Maybe a keen brain controls that drooling behemoth? Why don't Brainsville scientists know more about them?* OK, I realized that the scientific study of some huge ravenous beast wouldn't exactly be easy, but it was doable. Humans and Rangers even protected similar beasts on New Haven, according to Lonely Swimmer, my thesis adviser.

But Marcello didn't follow his own plan. I didn't even have time to dismount, let alone argue with him about the change in tactics. The girl fell from the tree. Some blister vines softened her fall, but she hit a few branches on the way down, smacked into the spongy ground from the forest floor, and became still. We approached the drooler at full speed as he slobbered over what he thought would be his next easy meal. I saw something metallic flash as Marcello leaped high, using those powerful hind legs to launch himself into the air like a champion horse in an equestrian contest on a low gravity planet. I hung on for dear life as he sailed over the beast and plunged something into the top of the drooler's head. We crashed to the ground, I jumped aside before Marcello crushed me in a body roll that softened the blow to himself. I stood and watched the drooler die.

"Check the girl," said Marcello, getting to his feet and shaking himself.

I was about to start that operation. A quick survey told me she was in bad shape. "She has a puncture wound, probably from a tree branch," I said, examining the girl. "Blister vine burns too. She's also unconscious. Maybe she has a concussion." I removed the jersey and studied the wound. "Just missed the heart. I'll keep pressure on it to control the bleeding if you take us to Middle Finger as fast as you can."

I had to rethink my plan too. There was no way I could apply pressure and mount Marcello carrying Natasha, so I had to go to plan B. I used my belt and shirt to serve as a clumsy pressure bandage. By that time, the girl was conscious. I comforted her for a few seconds and explained what had happened and what needed to be done. She bit her lower lip and nodded. Tough but sweet little thing, and with that brute of a father! Had to feel sorry for her.

"Climb on in front of me," I told Natasha after mounting Marcello. We both helped her get on board. "We're taking you to Middle Finger."

She hugged Marcello, as much for a thank you as for staying on board, I imagine, as he galloped toward the mining camp.

***

With their four legs, Fistians can run much faster than Humans. The correct verb is gallop, like a Kentucky Derby winner. (I'd read about that once and seen old still pictures, liking the horses much more than the finery all the women dressed up in.) I bet Marcello still set some records even for Fistians...or Kentucky thoroughbreds. We galloped into Middle Finger and skidded to a stop in front of Daniel Chang's tent. He came out with surprise etched on his weathered face.

"Natasha! Your father's out of his mind looking for you." She didn't respond. "What's wrong with her?"

"A puncture wound and maybe a concussion," I said.

"Take her inside. I'll get the doctor."

The camp's physician was more like a mechanic for rugged-terrain vehicles. He ran down what served as the camp's main street, pushing a porta-doc, and followed Chang into the tent. Pulling his suspenders into place, I saw grease-stained hands that matched the stains on shirt and pants.

"I hope you're going to wash up a bit," I said, wondering how many times he had worn that shirt. Its color was light enough to show sweat stains in the armpits too. If I'd come across him alone, I would have been scared of this wild man—more so at night.

He nodded. "Help me get the porta-doc in here," he said to Chang after a quick examination of the girl. "And you—" He pointed to Marcello. "—get out while you can. Today everyone here wants to kill a Fistian."

"He saved Natasha," I said in protest.

"They won't care, little girl. And you shouldn't try to reason with fanatics. You're that Fistian expert, right?" I nodded. "You need to get the hell out of town too. When that team comes back, they'll be looking for blood.

They'll choose yours and the centaur's if you're still around."

Chang nodded to me. "That's probably a good idea, Asako. I'll try to reason with them. Natasha is safe and sound. That's all that should matter to her father, but I don't know about the rest of them. No sense taking chances."

Marcello trotted out of town a lot slower than he came in, with me on his back. We were both deep in thought. I couldn't imagine what he was feeling about the thanks he got for saving Natasha. And I was wondering whether Humans should get off Hard Fist before it was too late. There was a lot of fanatical hate going around like a contagion that seemed to affect only Humans.

***

We stopped in a forest clearing where a spring fed a large pond. Marcello wanted to wash off the drooler's slobbers and blood. I wanted to clean up too.

I ducked my head under, swished my hair around to get out the sweat, and did the same to air-dry it. Not much luck there. It was very humid, especially in the woods. Saw one of the big four-winged insects eying me with curiosity. *Or hunger?* Never knew of one attacking a Human, but what did they eat? It was stretching its wings and preening, though, enjoying the heat and humidity. *Are these native insects intelligent? Does Hard Fist have more than one intelligent lifeform?* Didn't even know if insect was the right name. The word could mean so many things out among the stars. Some humans called Rangers water bugs, often a pejorative term I could never accept after meeting Lonely Swimmer.

Marcello was sitting on his butt in the water squeezing liquid from his mane. I floated.

"Did we do something wrong, Asako?"

"No, and maybe the miners will eventually realize that, if they ever return to their senses."

"Humans are illogical and emotional. Not you, of course."

I decided to change the topic. "Were you afraid of that drooler, Marcello?"

His eyebrows danced, meaning he found humor in the question, even given our situation.

"Of course. There are two reactions to fear: flight or fight. You don't have time to analyze. You react."

"That sounds a bit like a warrior's attitude." Again the dancing eyebrows. "Fistians seem so peaceful. There seems to be a contradiction here."

"We fight when we must. Otherwise, we're peaceful. But there's no diplomacy that works with a drooler."

"Agreed. But I ran, remember?"

"You reacted correctly, considering the situation. And that baby drooler lost the battle."

"I really didn't plan it that way."

"I know. Sometimes survival depends on some luck. We say that the ancestors smile on us when that happens."

OK, this is getting creepy. I really need to find out about these ancestors!

We let the water soothe away some of our mental and physical fatigue for a few moments. My friend seemed deep in thought. I decided to distract him.

"That was still very brave of you to go after the drooler that way."

"I had enough time to figure out he was fat and old and not very quick. It was his time to die. I didn't have to overthink what I needed to do. Didn't have time to do that anyway. He was about to eat the poor little Human."

"For such a big fellow, you can jump high and move quickly."

"Four strong legs let us jump and evolution has given us quick reflexes. But surprise was my friend. That drooler didn't have a chance as long as my aim with the spear was true."

Thought for a moment. "The miners won't have a chance if they attack, will they?"

"Not much, Asako. And we have the ancestors strategizing for us too."

Again those ancestors! It was as if the Fistians could talk to them. *Why don't they just come up with a peaceful solution if they're so damn smart?*

Could see the day when Humans would have to leave Hard Fist, though. Not a pleasant thought.

Chapter Twenty-One

I'd just returned to Brainsville when Daniel Chang, Boris Macar, and a few other miners showed up and demanded a meeting. Most scientists were out in the field. Only Karen McCarthy and my father were in town working in the Exogeology Lab. They invited me along, and we met the miners' delegation in the cafeteria. As we walked in, Macar's eyes drilled into me.

"What's she doing here?" he said while continuing the steamy glare in my direction. "This is an adult discussion. Kids don't belong here!"

"Seems like Asako has more right to be here than anyone," said Karen. "You should be happy to see one of two persons responsible for saving your daughter from a drooler." She had heard about our saving Natasha.

"They probably were just saving their own skins," said Boris. "And that Fistian is an animal, not a person."

"Now Boris, I warned you about being confrontational," said Daniel. "We talked about what we want to discuss with these folks. Asako is the most knowledgeable person around as far as Fistians are concerned."

"Let's get to that then," Dad2 said while Boris's face went from red to purple. "Karen, Asako, and I aren't official reps for the scientists, by the way. We can only pass on what you want to say to the whole group."

"OK by me," said Daniel. He looked at Boris and the other miners and waited. Macar was the last to nod. "What we want to propose is a relocation of the Fistian village, by force if necessary. We believe our difficulties with them are magnified by their proximity."

"Their difficulties caused by you miners, you mean," I said. "Sounds like a whiny way to cover up hateful xenophobia to me. And I bet that relocation will be upriver so you can get at those ore deposits below. You do know the Fistians fish in that river, its delta, and the ocean. If you contaminate all that, it doesn't matter where they move."

Boris ignored most of my little speech. "Are you calling me bigoted?" he said.

"An old saying is appropriate here," said Karen. "If the shoe fits, Macar, wear it."

Boris looked like she'd slapped him in the face, but he took it out on me. "Get that centaur-loving whelp out of here!" he said. "She's a trouble-maker."

"First, my centaur-loving whelp saved your daughter," said Dad2, "but one of those Fistians you hate did most of the saving. It was a team effort. Without Marcello's action, your daughter would be in the stomach of a drooler. Without Asako's, Natasha would have bled out even if the droller had lost interest." Dad2 pounded the table with his fist. "Second, pass this warning on to all the miners—the Fistians are an ancient civilization. They've been here a long time as near as we can tell. Centuries ago they exploited the rare earth deposits you covet, for example, but they halted that effort for whatever reason. They might be full of surprises if you attack them. Third, I'll pass on a description of your attitude to the other scientists. We have some psychs who can help you with your anger management. And fourth, this meeting is over." My father stood and looked at Karen and me. "Let's go breathe some fresh air. It's far too fouled in here."

Boris's face had progressively returned to its purple state as my father made his little speech. It was probably good to leave before he exploded. I was proud of Dad2. *But maybe too little, too late?*

***

Daniel Chang didn't leave with the scientists. He found us in the Exogeology Lab.

"Sorry about that. Boris really does need that course on anger management."

"No course could change his bigotry," I said. Karen and Dad2 nodded.

Daniel plopped into a spare chair. "What about ITUIP?" he said. "Could they do something?"

"Hard Fist isn't part of ITUIP, although this scientific expedition is, as part of that organization's general scientific efforts," said Karen. "Most of you miners are from planets outside ITUIP too. Sorry, they might hear us out and still do nothing; they'll ignore anything you request for the most part."

Karen looked haggard. Maybe she was realizing what her discovery of the rich ore deposits was leading to, or maybe she was worried that without ITUIP all the scientists would have to abandon their research on Hard Fist. A scientist about to lose years of hard work can never be a happy scientist.

"Besides, if Hard Fist were in ITUIP, the Protocol might apply, and all Humans would have to leave," said Dad2.

I thought that was a moot point. *Hard Fist isn't in ITUIP, so the Protocol is irrelevant.* I never expected my father to be a diplomatic genius, but he was being naïve. Or nervous, because he really didn't have anything to contribute as a solution? Like Karen, and probably Mom, he wouldn't want to lose years of scientific work.

"Let's be candid here," said Daniel. "If we forcefully try to resettle Fistians from the village, what will happen?"

"That's easy to answer," I said. "Miners will die just like that drooler did. You don't have the weapons for that fight. They have a tremendous advantage, maybe more than any of us realize."

"Let's ask the AI."

"I know what he'll say," said Karen. "Einstein, calculate the odds that Fistians will win a war with Humans here on Hard Fist."

"Asako Kobayashi needs to collect more data," said the computer.

"Do your best to make an estimate," said Dad2.

"Given current data, odds for the Fistians are twenty to one at least."

"What drives that conclusion if your data is insufficient?" said Daniel.

"Population estimates. They'll simply overwhelm the small number of Humans on Hard Fist."

My father smiled. "Einstein's calculation is conservative because the Fistian population is extrapolated from the initial surveys of our scientific expedition. We don't even know how many villages they have now—Asako says they come and go—or exactly where most of them are, for that matter."

Daniel shrugged. "I'm just someone who works with miners. What are the projections?"

"We need to do an accurate census, but the projections are around ten million," I said. "You only see this one village. They're all over Hard Fist."

"But aren't they very primitive? How could they organize?"

"You're thinking the villages are isolated and without communication?" I said. He nodded. "Don't think like that. In our local village, I met elders from several villages. There is some sort of communication system I don't quite understand yet, but it seemed Mama Dora's people knew the elders were coming and prepared to welcome them. One of them is her father who took me to another village, his own. The villages are settled and before they become too populated, they split, and a new village is created."

"Who's Mama Dora?"

"Clan mother for our local village."

Daniel frowned. "I guess there's a lot about Fistians I don't know. Are you implying that they just allowed us to come to Hard Fist out of the goodness of their hearts?"

"Yes. First scientists, now miners. They don't much care what we do as long as we leave them alone. What will happen if you don't isn't clear, but you have Einstein's guess. That goodness in their hearts might rapidly evaporate. They're not pushovers, Daniel. My friend Marcello took down an adult drooler with some kind of spear. Would you like to try to equal that feat?"

Daniel shuddered. "I'd prefer not to even think about it because I'd probably fail. All right, what do you three propose?"

"A wait-and-see period," said my father. "At the first opportunity, we'll make an official query to the ITUIP. I think I can predict their answer, though."

"And that would be?"

"It's not ITUIP's problem," said Karen. "They might make the suggestion to resolve your issues with Fistians, or leave their planet. It is *their* planet, by the way."

"The miners will never accept that, but I can try to convince them to wait for the official word."

145

Daniel shook our hands and left.

***

"Poor guy is caught in a difficult situation," said Karen. "What's going to happen?"

"We might be in a more difficult situation," Dad2 said. "Too many of us don't like Fistians either. They are a bit aloof and haughty, you know. But I can't see myself supporting the miners."

"You think they're aloof and haughty because you don't understand them," I said. "They're my friends. The aloofness is only because they don't trust us completely for some reason, and they're discovering more reasons for that with every day that passes. They're not haughty either. They've been around a long time and know things. Call it cultural pride. For example, their ancestors told them to put the village where they did. They would be going against the wishes of those ancestors if they moved, thereby disrespecting them."

"Sorry, that does sound primitive," said Karen. "I'll have to ask Swensen, but 'speaking to ancestors' characterized a lot of pre-historic Earth societies, I believe."

"I understand it to mean a direct dialog, Karen. And those ancestors might be responsible for the planet-wide communication. I need to learn a lot more about them."

My father nodded. "But there might not be time for that."

Chapter Twenty-Two

"Tell your captain my partner and I would like to invite her to dinner," Lars Swenson said to the head of security of the starship *Reliant*. Lars, my father, and I were helping to confirm delivery of some much needed supplies and equipment to the Brainsville scientists. "She and I were old SEB shipmates years ago."

ITUIP's Space Exploration Bureau had many duties, one being discovering new planets where ITUIP's citizens could colonize. Its ships generally contained mixed crews. But all the scientists on Hard Fist were SEB employees too, carrying out various research programs that helped inform those decisions made about colonization. Hard Fist had always been considered unsuitable for colonization because of its large native population, but studies still continued, just more oriented to scientific knowledge. Dad2 always said we weren't high on SEB's priority list because of that, and there was always some budget guru somewhere ready to make cuts.

I smiled at what Lars had just said. Probably at the time he was talking about being shipmates with *Reliant*'s captain, all scientists not from the three original Earth colonies were SEB scientists. Nowadays many were also affiliated with universities, but there were still many SEB scientists around, including bureaucrats—maybe it isn't appropriate to call them scientists? I didn't understand much of the politics involved in scientific research but figured my time would come soon enough.

"Janice has some formal gathering in Middle Finger," said the crewman, "but I'll send your regards. She took a flitter there right after our shuttle landed."

Dad2 looked at me and frowned, and then he glared at the crewman. "You said formal gathering? She's not visiting friends?"

The crewman shrugged. "Don't know why she'd be friends with any of those miners. They have nothing to do with ITUIP. Most of them come from out-worlds. Some mining bigwigs came in on another shuttle, though. They have a big ship in orbit. I think she's talking to them. Something about transfer of authority, I believe. That's about all the info I have."

We spent the rest of the day doing inventory. Later on at home, Dad2 offered me some wine before dinner. I saw my mother's raised eyebrows.

"Asako's too young," she said.

"She deserves it. She worked hard today. Everyone but Lars was out in the field."

"That old man theorizes too much. He should be out in the field with Asako studying Fistian ruins and figuring out their cultural origins."

"The thesis has to be my own work, Mom."

"The exosociological part. No one's looked at the exoarchaeological part besides Lars. Your father finds abandoned villages in ruin and wide areas full of Fistian-made shards. Someone should be helping Lars make sense of all that."

Again I thought of the ancestors. "Any idea how old the ruins are?"

"Ancient, like I told Macar, and that's Lars's opinion." Dad2 shrugged. "Not my area of expertise. They're old, though. I find some of them below lava fields and strata."

"Makes me wonder," I said. "Maybe Fistian civilization is a lot older than people realize. Ancient might describe it, but that's imprecise."

Mom surprised me with a historical shtick. "Humans on Earth went through what you'd call many civilizations. I believe the oldest overall was the Mesopotamian. The oldest one in the American continents was the Mayan. Your father probably has Incan blood; the Incan civilization dominated western South America for years."

"More Japanese blood than Incan, I'm sure. Someone way back there probably was Incan, but Peru had a lot of Japanese immigrants.

"I've heard about all those civilizations," I said, "but it seems that Fistian civilizations are planet-wide and all come and go in sequence and not just here and there on Hard Fist. That's all I've heard so far. Maybe Lars could help me understand that aspect because it could be sociologically important."

"I have first dibs on Lars," said my father. "I've asked him to corral Janice Houston and find out what she was discussing with the miners."

***

Lars's announcement was troubling. "Janice didn't know the situation, and the mining moguls made a good argument: the miners form the largest group of Humans on Hard Fist. From her viewpoint, it was logical to transfer the authority from us to the miners."

My father's fist crashed onto the kitchen table, making the tea service jump—reminded me of the meeting with Macar. "ITUIP has no legal authority to do that!"

Lars frowned. "They do now. The miners are petitioning for membership in ITUIP."

"They'll never follow ITUIP rules," I said. "That's a ruse to wrest authority from us and allow them to do what they want to the Fistians. And your Janice should have seen right through that ploy!"

"We're technically not ITUIP either," said Lars with a shrug, "just SEB employees for the most part and not all from ITUIP planets by any means. This probably wouldn't have happened if she knew the situation on the planet as well as we do. She can't see why Fistians can't relocate, by the way."

"Because she doesn't know Fistians," I said. "No one does, not even me. But this is their planet, not the miners'. I guarantee you that Fistians far outnumber all Humans on this planet. Why do Humans think they have the right to take, take, take?"

Lars looked sheepish. "I'll have to admit that I didn't tell Janice how many Fistians live on Hard Fist. That might have changed her mind. It's the argument against making this a Human colony, after all."

My mother, who had been listening to the discussion, decided to make a related point. "There's never been a case where a minority Human population on a planet has forced a majority non-Human one to join ITUIP. Where that has happened, the non-Human population wanted to join as much as the Human one."

"We have to change that captain's mind. As the local ITUIP rep, she can do that, can't she?"

"*Reliant* already left orbit. But we can send word on the next one. They'd never approve the miners' petition without consulting Fistians."

"The miners never wanted that," I said. "It's all a ruse. They're stalling."

***

"We'd heard," said Marcello after I told him what happened. His tail was swishing, but there were no flies. He was mad. "We are now preparing for war. This will make our preparations all the more urgent."

"That's silly. We'll all be losers then. What would I do? What would you do?" I was about ready to cry.

"More and more elders are coming around to the idea that war is inevitable. I'd have to side with my own people. I don't know what you will do."

"Oh, sweet *Magellan*. Take me for a ride." I'd learned that expression on Sanctuary. Marcello probably didn't recognize the historical reference, but it was a good expression to use in place of stronger words I felt like uttering. It referred to the old colonizing ship Humans and Rangers had turned into the first FTL starship.

As we rode swiftly through the forest and across wide paddocks with their tall grass, I pretended I was on that starship among those colonists bound for New Haven, one of the original three Earth colonies. First contact had been made with the strange people Humans now called Rangers. That had gone so well. *Why can't it go as well on Hard Fist?*

I caught glimpses of Big Fellow, a pastel ghost filling half of Hard Fist's sky, its stormy bands chasing around its girth like they do on gas giants everywhere. I buried my head in Marcello's mane and longed for simpler days.

The ride strengthened my resolve. I could never support Humans in a war against Fistians. I'd go and join Mama Dora's clan before I did that. *Will I be considered a traitor to my own people? Will my parents disown me?*

I'd never seen a furious Fistian. At the worst, they just ignored me. Would that attitude worsen when fighting began? I hoped not. I loved Marcello like a brother, but I wouldn't want to cause him problems…or any harm.

A.B. CAROLAN

PART V:
THE SECRET
OF THE URNS

A.B. CAROLAN

Chapter Twenty-Three

When Marcello and I returned to his village, Mama Dora invited me to her place for dinner. Deciding I needed to earn it by doing something constructive, I offered to get water from the cistern. I was going there anyway because I was thirsty, and the day had been unusually hot. The fresh spring water beckoned me. Marcello, who had been lathered in sweat and bathed, offered to help.

The water looked so inviting that I cupped my hands and drank. Splashed a bit on my face too. Because I was dressed skimpily, I felt like jumping in the cistern. Knew I'd still feel hot when I got out, though, and thought it wasn't a good idea to pollute it with my perspiration. We filled the huge buckets and returned to Mama Dora's abode.

As I helped prepare the meager dinner all Fistians like—it was reminiscent of salty mush prepared from grain, except the grain was wild and harvested from grasses on the higher mountain slopes—I continued quizzing Mama Dora and Marcello about Fistian culture. *How many Fistians are there? What's the nexus between clans? Who are the ancestors? How do they talk to them?* When I tried to home in on answers, I was detoured, sometimes by Mama Dora, others times by Marcello.

"Are you being circumspect because I'm Human?"

"Your question, Marcello," said Mama Dora. "I need to mix the contents for the spice tray."

She went outside with a large bowl and a plate with multiple compartments. Each one would contain different spice mixes I'd learned to sprinkle on the bland mush to make it more enjoyable after I scooped it out. There were breakfast spices and dinner spices—they generally didn't eat lunch. Some dinner ones were strong enough to bring tears to my eyes and burn all the way down my throat, so I avoided those, but I ran a risk—sometimes Mama Dora slipped in some new mixtures I didn't recognize.

"I know what you're doing," said Marcello. "So does Mama Dora. I'll be candid. You're not Fistian enough to know all our secrets, Asako."

I studied Marcello to see if he was being nasty. He shimmered and faded in and out, like a mirage in the hot sun, but I knew Mama Dora's hovel wasn't that hot. In fact, it was designed to catch any breeze that was available and was generally cooler than outside.

Dizziness overcame me and I fell. Marcello was quick enough to break the fall and not let my head hit the hard ground.

"Mama Dora!"

***

I remember a deluge of words in the Fistian language between Mama Dora, Marcello, and other Fistians who had come running. Mama Dora made me sit up enough to drink something bitter. It made me vomit. After feeling embarrassed, I passed out.

When I woke up, I heard my mother's voice. I'd already sensed her presence in my pre-awakening stupor. She was small, compact, and always struggling with her weight, but there always seemed to be this aura around her that I had felt since I was a tiny baby. That aura was as big as Mama Dora's—two very different mother figures that were important in my young life.

I wiped tears from my eyes and then realized I couldn't see. *What happened?* The last thing I remembered was drinking refreshing water that in hindsight had tasted a bit weird. I tried to place that taste and decided it was a strong taste like the water in Lonely Swimmer's tank on Sanctuary. *Some chemical?*

"Getting her to vomit probably saved her," Mom said.

"The water had a peculiar odor," said Mama Dora. "It might have become fouled with bacteria. I've told everyone in the village to stop drinking it."

Didn't Marcello drink some?

"Are any of you sick?" Mom said, nearly echoing my thought.

"I made Marcello vomit too. We don't know anyone else who drank from there recently, but it's a communal resource."

"We'll have to make some tests. If this well is fed by an underground spring, how could the water become polluted? It looks fine." *I couldn't see anything!* I still imagined her holding up some test tubes by the clinks of glass on glass I heard. "I'll have to take these back to my lab and test the water. Can Asako stay here?"

"Of course. I will take good care of her, Mother of the First Born. I dumped the food, by the way, so we'll go hungry tonight. I used cistern water to boil the grain. When you return tomorrow, you should bring some of her favorite dishes. We'll be fasting until we know your conclusions." *Wait a minute! Can't you ask the ancestors?* "You'll have them before we do."

"You can perform tests?" said Mom.

"Our only but thorough test must be done elsewhere. It would take a while, so you're the first option. Please hurry. The sooner we know, the better."

I was blind and starving. *What a state to be in!*

A few minutes later, a shaman visited me. All he did was hold my hand and chant a bit, but it was comforting. So was Marcello.

"This is most unusual," said the shaman. "That water comes from underground and feeds into the river. It's always been pure since we discovered the spring."

"Exactly where is the spring?" I said. "It's not under the well, right?"

"It's some distance from the village. We laid ceramic pipe. Before that, we had to boil the water from the other well."

"So someone could poison the water at its source?"

Am I being paranoid? After the confrontations with the miners, I thought I had a right to be.

"Are you suggesting a Human tried to poison our water supply?"

"Tried and succeeded, I fear."

***

I was right. When Mom showed up with test results the next morning, she came with Lars Swensen and Dad2.

"There's a high level of chlorine and chlorine reactants in the samples," Mom said. "Also some rare earth residues. Asako probably would have vomited on her own unless the contaminants killed her outright. Her blindness should be temporary too."

"We don't use chlorine," said Mama Dora. "What could be its source?"

I sat up. "Miners use it to keep their water supplies free from bacteria," I said.

"Exactly what I was thinking," said Dad2. "I told Lars as much."

Lars nodded. "I'm afraid the war has begun."

"War?" said Mama Dora. "This is not war. We do not fight this way. What other poisonous chemicals will they attack us with?"

She was wrong, of course. Although Fistians weren't familiar with chemical warfare, it had been practiced on Earth even during the early days before spaceflight, and the materials used were often a lot worse than chlorine. Sarin gas, for example, was used a lot after it was developed.

"It's a mining camp," I said. "They have all kinds, including radioactive waste from the rare-earth mining."

"I'll have to confront Daniel and his friends," said Lars. "Never trusted that guy."

I didn't want to be at that confrontation. I imagined the worst. *Will miners attack the scientists?* Neither Lars nor my parents were skilled in self-defense, and if miners used guns, they could die. I was becoming an emotional wreck, but that felt justified after what happened to me.

"We'll go with you," said my parents.

Chapter Twenty-Four

I learned about my parents' and Lars's visit to Middle Finger afterwards from my father. The following is a synopsis....

"They're in the pub," Daniel told them. "Couldn't figure out why they had anything to celebrate, but now I know. I'll give you company."

Boris Macar and his buddies were already well along the road to complete intoxication.

"What you doing with those centaur lovers, Daniel?" said Macar.

Mom held up a large bottle she had Marcello draw from the Fistian well. "Fistians think everything on this planet is a gift from their ancestors. They sent this bottle of pure spring water as a gift toward peace and understanding between Fistians and Humans. Can I add a bit to your whiskey?"

Boris blanched. So did several others. "We drink our whiskey neat," said Boris. His glass was empty, but other glasses had watered-down whiskey in them.

"Drink the water straight too, then, in honor of the peace process."

"Drinking water won't lead to peace between us," said one of Boris's companions, his voice almost a growl.

"You would dishonor their gift?" said Daniel. "Their intentions are good."

"No, they're not!" said Boris. "They're trying to kill us."

"Why'd you do it?" Dad2 said, getting right to the crux of the matter.

"Do what?"

"You just as much admitted you poisoned their water supply! And you did it right at the source."

"By the way, it wasn't enough to kill Fistians," Mom said.

"There you go. It was just a warning. No harm done."

"No harm done? You didn't count on my daughter Asako drinking that water, did you?" Dad2 said. Mom had become so angry at that point that she was red and couldn't talk. "You're not just stupid. You're ignorant and a danger to everyone."

"It's what your damn daughter deserves for being a centaur lover."

That's when Mom threw the water bottle at him.

***

A fight then broke out between miners and the three scientists, with Daniel trying to break it up. He received a concussion from a bottle smashed on his head and a broken arm for his good intentions. Lars and my parents were holding their own, mostly because the miners were so drunk they could hardly stand up erect. They would take a swing, miss, and fall on the floor.

The fight was stopped by a chorus of war cries that shook all the windows in the pub. The fighters went outside to see ten young Fistians galloping up the mining camp's main street; they were armed with spears. The Fistian warriors had painted their faces white, but they'd put dark bands under their eyes as if the bright sun would ruin the aim of their weapons. They were all Marcello's age and in great physical shape. When I heard this, I again thought, *these miners don't know what they're getting into!*

From my studies on Sanctuary, I knew that intelligent beings who live close to the land value physical prowess, but they also value intelligence. Both are necessary to become the dominant species on a planet. That seemed to be the common denominator for all evolution, physical and cultural, because with intelligence comes cooperation where the greater good of a group goes hand-in-hand with physical prowess.

The miners were unarmed so they could only stare as Marcello separated from the group, came to an abrupt halt in front of Boris Macar, and buried his spear at the miner's feet.

"We are now at war, Human!"

He turned and the ten galloped out of town, sounding their war cries.

The miners were speechless. The three scientists were shaking their heads.

"Now look at what you've done," Dad2 said to Boris, wiping blood from his eyes that had come from a gash above his eyebrow. "And I don't blame them. I hope you don't get any sleep at night with the realization that you might become responsible for the massacre of every Human on this planet, including children—your child too! By the way, that Fistian was the one who saved your little girl Natasha from the drooler!"

"And I would have shot him if I had a gun!" said Boris. "Let's arm ourselves, men. If they want war, they'll get war. Next stop for us is the Fistian village!"

Mom had gone inside the pub to check on Daniel. Lars and Dad2 joined her.

"We have to stop them," she said.

"Good luck with that," said Lars. "I think we need to make plans to leave Hard Fist. There's no way we can defend ourselves against a mob of angry miners. Or millions of Fistians. Things could get ugly very fast. And we really have no business taking sides."

Chapter Twenty-Five

While all that was going on, I was feeling worse. Mama Dora was getting desperate. She called in one of the village's elders.

"Can you test for radioactive material?" she said in the Fistian language. *What? Hadn't Mom made that test?* It then occurred to me that Mom's discovery of rare earth compounds didn't preclude radioactive isotopes. *Do I have radiation poisoning too?*

If I had been thinking clearly, I would have felt proud that I understood some of what Mama Dora had said. By that time in my studies of Fistian culture, I could catch a few words and phrases. I was sure that the three Fistian words literally translated as "particle emitting substances" was just their way of saying "radioactive material," for example.

I made a mental list of symptoms. Maybe the poison had weakened me and still was a bit active, but most of the symptoms matched her diagnosis.

The elder bowed and left. He soon returned with the shaman who carried a huge glass ball with a cork on top. It was filled with a milky vapor. He put it against my breast and studied it for a moment. He then put it next to the water and studied that.

He shook his head sadly.

***

I later learned a bit more about Fistian shamans. The village shaman has a curious role. The traditional mumbo-jumbo was more secular than religious, more poetry and song than trying to cast a spell or drive out

163

demons that cause sickness, and more psychological than medical. In short, a shaman is a bit like the fool or joker in an old European courts; he tries to make everyone happy and feel better.

But he also had some practical knowledge. He could smooth muscle aches and pains away because he knew anatomy; he could dress wounds and splint broken limbs; and he could recommend natural potions that fixed inside ills too.

He always goes to the patient. He's usually very sociable in playing that role. He's akin to an old frontier doctor in Earth's Old West, an area that became part of that old country, the United States, often credited with starting the serious exploration of outer space.

The shaman is the second most powerful figure in a village and works closely with the clan mother. Mama Dora was no exception, and it was clear she valued his opinions. Marcello had a bit more modern attitude. I knew he didn't consider the shaman a scientist. Many people would also consider my special friend Doc, for example, more an artisan than a scientist, so that didn't bother me. I'd seen on Sanctuary that only medical doctors with additional degrees did medical research. People who use scientific knowledge don't have to be scientists, after all.

I didn't even know if exosociology is a science. They'd been debating that for centuries. So much of it depended on opinions, but all scientists start from data and try to make sense of it, and that last part has to contain opinions. Fortunately I didn't have to make predictions about Fistian behavior. *Or would I?* You never know when someone will call you an expert and put you on the spot!

***

Mama Dora bent over me. "It's more than chlorine, Asako. There's only one recourse. Hop on top of me like you do with Marcello. We're going for a ride." She nodded to the village elder and the shaman. "Marcello has delivered our challenge. Prepare our defenses. And send him to the grotto when he returns."

I understood that perfectly. Fistians were going to war with my people, and I was helpless to do anything about it.

Chapter Twenty-Six

I started to feel delirious as I tried to stay conscious and hold on tight to Mama Dora's mane. The rainforest became a multi-colored blur of green and brown. Soon I dreamed I was back in the village...

The Fistians were in a celebratory mood as I left Marcello's hut and ran to where they were gathered. I ran so fast that I had to hold onto the wildflowers braided into my hair. I bowed to them all, but more deeply to Mama Dora, and I remained that way.

Doc approached more sedately. The Fistian wedding ceremony began.

I could hardly wait for it to finish, even though I felt honored that Mama Dora had agreed to officiate. When the brief ceremony was over and I ran away with Doc, my heart was beating with excitement.

In some hut we'd borrowed, not Marcello's, Doc lowered me gently onto some Fistian cushions and kissed me. I would be ravished by him again. But as he straddled me, he became the brutish Boris Macar. I screamed....

"Hush, First Born," said Mama Dora. "We're almost there."

"We need to save both the Human scientists and the Fistians from the miners!"

"I know, I know. But first things first. I know what must be done. Trust me."

Of course I will. *How can I not?* I thought of how close I was to Marcello, Mama Dora, and Drel. They were as much a part of my family as Mom and Dad2. Doc seemed far away.

"Where are we going?"

"It is time for you to meet our ancestors. Patience, Asako."

***

Mama Dora bowed at the cave entrance and then carried me inside in her strong arms. It wasn't dark but lit with bioluminescent walls. My hand glowed when I touched one. That soft light seemed to stop the freezing air from sapping all my body heat.

"Old technology," said Mama Dora. "I'd rather this not be the way I introduce you to our ancestors, Asako. I don't know if they can save you either. In fact, they might kill you."

"They're here?" I'd climbed on her back again, gripping her mane. "Where?"

"Patience, little First Born."

We trotted along the cave's sandy floor, winding lower and lower for several hundred meters. The cold became more intense, although it was warmer than being outside in the open on Hard Fist at night. But I was sick, so maybe that made me feel the cold more. It didn't seem to bother Mama Dora. Fistians didn't like to be out and about on a cold night either, but I'd learned they could handle the extreme temperature swings better than Humans.

We entered a huge grotto, stalactites and stalagmites joining to form huge, multicolored dew-covered columns that seemed to be supporting the ceiling of an ancient and wonderful Earth cathedral. No Human cathedral could compare, though. Still, that perception was partly justified by thousands of glowing funeral urns that filled the cavern. At least, that's what I thought they were.

My astonishment was heightened when the music started. Not the raucous music of Fistians' lively partying at Mama Dora's village or the wedding celebration in Drell's. This was more ethereal like Drel's singing on the raft, only there were many Fistian voices, hundreds of them, creating something akin to a choral piece without words. *And they're all in my head!*

After putting me down, Mama Dora joined in for a bit, bowing to all points of the compass. Her voice was the only one not in my head, but it blended well with them. Palestrina and other old Human composers who had written choral music I loved would have been envious. I felt my nape hair standing on end.

Several tens of urns then became brighter. She arranged them in concentric circles and put me into their center. Three rings of those brighter urns surrounded me. I felt at peace with the universe. *Is this magic? Or a religious ceremony?* I didn't think my radiation poisoning would be solved by either magic or religion.

The urns began to sing a different song. Mama Dora joined in that one too. I started to feel queasy and collapsed.

***

My parents told me later about what had happened back at the village. Because of the impending war, they and a few other scientists decided to go to the village and take me to safety, away from any potential hostilities. They were certain Fistians wouldn't attack Brainsville before they attacked mining communities. Some also believed the miners would soon surrender and it would all be over. But they wanted me out of harm's way, neither in the Fistian village nor in Middle Finger.

Nice of them. They'd been aloof at best and hostile to Fistians at worst, even before the miners had arrived. For many of the scientists, I was probably just that annoying little girl who insisted on playing with Marcello…if they even bothered to think about me. I'm sure the ones who came with my parents wouldn't have without them pleading for help.

When they arrived, they couldn't get in. Everything looked normal. They could see the Fistian clan going about their business—tending vegetable gardens, preparing meals, weaving baskets, making new cooking ware, conversing or singing, and so forth. The Fistians ignored the Humans, even when my parents jumped up and down and waved.

When they tried to enter the village, it seemed like the air would shimmer, sizzle, and then become resistant. Dad2 said that's when they finally concluded they didn't know enough about Fistians because the shield was like the defensive ones on all but the smallest ITUIP starships. I'd seen how those were set up on that spacewalk with Doc, but I hadn't seen it in action. That was probably fortunate because I would have been hurled off the hull into space, maybe to burn up in Nirvana's atmosphere.

I thought a shield to protect Fistian villages was a clever idea. How they did that was a mystery—there wasn't any ship's hull to support it. Its existence told me that maybe the miners were probably not only outnumbered but outmatched.

***

I awoke with Marcello stroking my hair. It felt almost as stringy and lifeless as I did. I was bathed in a cold sweat and felt nauseous. "Where-where am I?"

"In one of our ancestral caves," he said. "Mama Dora is out and about looking for fresh fruit for you. She'll bring back gourds of water too. I wanted to do that, but she says the ancestors suggested some special berries that will help speed up your recovery. I'd never heard of them." He took my hand. "But I think you're out of danger now."

"They-they cured my radiation sickness?"

His eyebrows raised—his smile. "You knew?"

"I've learned some words from your language. Probably more than you wanted me to learn. And the shaman looked worried." I looked sideways into the grotto and saw the glowing urns. The concentric circles were still there, but the urns in the inner circles were no longer brighter than the others. "Are your ancestors in the urns?"

"Their essences are stored there. It's complicated. Most of us don't understand the technology anymore. Think of them like information stored in your computers. Only a few elders understand the technology used, and only shamans know how to use that knowledge to preserve the ancestors' essences. Someday I hope to understand the technology, among many other things."

"What happened to Fistians? How did such an advanced culture become so simple?"

"Let's just say we fight a lot when the planet is crowded. The survivors return to a simpler life. And then we do it all over again. The Humans have interrupted that cycle. Now we'll wage war against them and not among ourselves. Maybe the cycle will forever be broken."

"Neither one is good," I said. "We have to try to stop it."

"I'm open to suggestions."

Chapter Twenty-Seven

After a simple repast of berries and water—breakfast? dinner? who knew?—I was allowed to meet some ancestors. Marcello suggested it. Mama Dora agreed I was ready. I wasn't so sure. I'd read ghost stories. The ancestors seemed like ghosts. And ordinary people often weren't treated well by ghosts in those stories.

But my reluctance had its less ghostly side. It was a bit like visiting a clinic or hospital for a test you've never done before. Often the stress before the test is worse than the test itself. *Will this be similar?* That new test would at least be administered by Human doctors—these doctors would be neither Human nor Fistian. Not knowing what they were and what the test would be made it even worse.

"Be forewarned, little one. Before they only affected your body. Now they will touch your mind."

Yeah, that did it! My previous apprehension was magnified. I didn't think the ancestors would hurt me— not intentionally, at least. But would they make me less Human and more Fistian? *What does "touch your mind" mean?* Again I thought of ghosts and the paranormal stories I'd read just for fun as a kid.

I'd eaten outside the grotto in bright sunlight because I was cold. Now Marcello, not Mama Dora, carried me back inside. Entering the cave made me feel cold again. I rubbed my arms, now feeling a chill, as Marcello moved slower. We were soon among the urns. Again circles were made with me in the center. Again I fell into a trance-like state alongside Marcello, but a fuzzy presence took hold of my mind as my vision turned inwards and I met some ancestors. The sensations weren't that bad. In fact, it was like the good feeling you might have when you encounter old friends you haven't seen in a while.

The first one seemed female. I felt a buzzing inside my head and then a Fistian voice. "I will not hurt you, Asako. I am a historian. Let me teach you some of our history."

There were few words as the eventful scenes from centuries of Fistian history flew into my head and remained lodged in my memories. Marcello was wrong. *Or did he mislead me?* The Fistians didn't fight that much among themselves—certainly less than Humans had throughout Earth's history. They just couldn't agree on what to do about the Marauders.

I'd written reports for school on Pearl Harbor and the Holocaust, for example. Couldn't remember which scientists back in camp were interested in Earth history. When your teachers are many, sometimes your education becomes one big blur, but enough scientists had been interested in teaching history with the help of the camp's AI.

At first Hard Fist's history paralleled Earth's—an expansion of Fistians across their solar system and then on to the nearest stars where they eventually ran up against a warring people they called Marauders—that's as good a translation as any of the Fistian word. Many times they had to retreat to Hard Fist where the Marauders left them alone for centuries for some unknown reason. Every time Fistians expanded their influence beyond their solar system, though, the same thing happened.

I formed a mental picture of the people who had once been a nemesis for both Humans and Rangers but were now partners in ITUIP. "Why haven't we met these Marauders?" I said. "Were they the Tali?" My questions were vocalized, but I knew the answers wouldn't be. I'd "hear it" all the same. *Eerie!*

"No. The Marauders are different. Because I can't physically go see if they're still around, I don't know if they even exist anymore. Perhaps they don't. Perhaps there isn't any reason for us to stay confined to Hard Fist now. But let me now describe some more of the experiences we had with the Marauders...."

***

The description was mostly via more images—a pictorial history left in my mind. The ancestors soon became a mental choir where all contributed to my stereotypical image of a Marauder. Like the Tali, they were a bit ursine, but they were even taller than a full-grown male Fistian. The beak and wings reminded me of a big furry Earth bird, but I couldn't give a name to it with the cacophony going on in my head. When studying Earth's flora and fauna you now generally studied extinct species, some extinctions caused by Humans and others later by the Tali.

There were action images too, mostly of the wholesale slaughter of Fistians. The Marauder leaders often made an example of Fistian leaders by biting off their heads with that powerful beak. I started to get queasy. *Such carnage!* No wonder the Fistians hated them.

The Marauders also seemed to have an FTL drive of their own because whole fleets of ships would pop back into our universe already in orbit around their target planet where they subsequently pillaged and killed. Didn't know how they did that. Our ships can't jump into or out of their FTL drive modes close to a star like that because of the strong gravity well. Most starship trips are 20-30% in and out of a solar system, and the rest is tiptoeing through metaverses, all carefully controlled by AIs.

There were legends about ET races living in and using something called the Nexus, something that linked all those metaverses together. Most scientists thought Swarm, that collective intelligence filling an entire globular cluster, partly lived in the Nexus. I thought that meant we who lived in near-Earth space still had a lot to learn about physics, but that still didn't make hard sciences attractive to me.

"Excuse me," said the original female Fistian ancestor. "A companion wants to talk to you one-on-one."

Talk? I felt another presence in my mind. "I am a scientist, Asako. I suggested your cure to Mama Dora and the shaman. That was made easier once the shaman explained that the radiation probably came from some of our rare earth isotopes. Long ago when we mined them, it was necessary to come up with such cures for radiation sickness."

"We want to warn you before we get onto science and off the topic of Marauders," said the first ancestor, interrupting her companion—I sensed the second's irritation. *Maybe she thinks the scientist's explanation is a moot point?* Neither they nor the choir had seemed as compassionate as when I was cured of radiation sickness. "There are Fistians who conflate Humans with Marauders and are ready to kill you all. You'll have to convince them there are no Marauders, or that you're certainly not them."

On and on it went. At times I felt my head would explode, and I thought I'd go crazy before it all ended. But, after it was all over, they were all gone from my mind, yet all the memories remained.

And I then knew what I had to do.

***

"Ready to go back?" said Marcello.

"To the village?"

"No. Mama Dora and I have one job to do with our people, you have another with yours. I'll take you to Brainsville's limits."

"I'm still a bit queasy. That would be helpful. Thanks. I feel like I was talking to those ancestors forever. What an experience!"

Mama Dora's eyebrows danced this time, showing her amusement. "It was for only five or so of your minutes, little one. You Humans would say the information transfer rate is high. It would be even faster, but your wi-fi implant seems to get in the way a bit. Does your head hurt?"

"Yes, I have the mother of all headaches. Even the sensory input is overwhelming. I'm awed by the whole experience." I hugged her. "Thank you for curing the radiation sickness."

"Thank the ancestors. And for the rest, I too was awed so many of your centuries ago. Awed and humbled. That first time is intense. And you were still weak from the treatment. I'm glad the experiment was successful. It's the first time a non-Fistian has met our ancestors."

Thought about that a bit. I still felt Human, but now I understood Fistians better than ever. I'd have to be selective in my thesis—I had information overload! And maybe some of that information shouldn't be divulged. But an urgent thought made those ruminations seem almost irrelevant.

"Are you going to convince your people to stop the war?"

"They're cautious by nature, so right now they'll hide behind their shields. But yes, we have to start working on that. Convincing those among us who equate you to

Marauders won't be easy, especially those who live in far-away villages. Humans look so much like them."

I accessed my mental picture of a Marauder. "Not really. Bipeds, yes, with some similar features. Those are common enough in near-Earth space. Fistians are more exceptional."

"In many ways," said Marcello, his eyebrows dancing. "Are you ready to ride?"

***

On that ride to Brainsville on Marcello's back, I organized my thoughts, deciding how much of my experience I could or should relate to my parents and the other scientists. I needed to do some of that because those Humans itching for a fight needed to understand that Fistians in their own way are just as advanced as we are. Maybe more so. But how could I prove any of it without violating the reverence and awe I now felt for the Fistians' ancestors? There was no clear path for me, but I thought it would be impossible to completely describe my experience with the ancestors no matter what I decided.

At the Brainsville limits, I gave Marcello a goodbye hug. "If things get really bad, we might not see each other again."

I had tears in my eyes. I don't know if they were there because of my firmness about knowing what I had to do, even if I didn't know how to do it; the breathless ride from the cave at full gallop, holding on to Marcello's mane for fear of falling; or the thought that it might be the last time I would be with my best friend, which would mean I'd never ride with him again!

"We have to work hard so that won't happen," he said. "But, if it does, you will always be welcome in our village. You're just a Fistian in Human form now, you know. The ancestors have accepted you as one of ours."

I wiped away tears. "I-I'll hold you to that, old friend."

I watched him trot away. *If we are successful, I'll have one hell of a thesis! If not, could I ever live with myself?*

A.B. CAROLAN

PART VI:
A PEACEFUL
RESOLUTION

A.B. CAROLAN

Chapter Twenty-Eight

I found it easier to convince my parents than some other scientists that war between Fistians and Humans was ill-advised. Led by Sam Rivers, the others balked. Sam, in particular, couldn't be convinced that Fistian technology was superior to ours in many ways. He hadn't been stopped by the shield, for example. I couldn't really blame him. Fistians seemed to be placid savages who lived an agrarian life in their small clans. I wasn't about to mention either ancestors or their urns—the doubters would believe that even less, so why bother?

Although I was cured, I didn't have all that much energy to argue with them either. I was drained by the events in the grotto and those leading up to it. What turned the tide, for me and the other Human scientists, was an ultimatum from the miners, all those on Hard Fist, not just those in Middle Finger: Either Fistians agreed to relocate their villages when Humans (meaning miners) considered it necessary, or there would be war.

"They're just a bunch of bullies," I said to those gathered around our kitchen table.

"I'll argue about that," said Mom. "That's too nice a word for anyone that condones poisoning an entire population. If we were on an ITUIP planet, they'd be tried and condemned to serve time on a prison planet."

"I've never supported the existence of those planets," said Dad2, "but now I'm changing my mind. Some people can't be reformed and will always be violent and/or psychotic."

"We pardoned the Tali," said Lars, "and they collectively reformed. Swarm was going to destroy them. We argued against that."

"And we and the Rangers had really good reasons to support Swarm's decision," I said, "considering all their crimes, but we didn't. Fortunately Swarm listened." That was all ancient history, of course, but I'd learned some history in school. "But I'd still like to try to convince miners that they are in a no-win situation here. Fistians will use all the ancestors' knowledge to defeat them. I told you that many hardliners among them identify us with the Marauders."

"I've never seen any evidence that these Marauders ever existed," said Lars.

"The galaxy is vast," Dad2 said. "We've only explored near-Earth systems. We don't know what or who else is out there. And we probably don't want to meet those Marauders any more than angry Fistians if they're like the worst Humans."

Karen McCarthy was studying me. "They cured you of radiation sickness, Asako. How'd they do that?"

I felt a bit trapped. "Physics? Magic?" I didn't want to dwell on the how, but I could justify avoiding the question because I didn't understand the process at all. It's one thing to experience something; it's another to understand it. "What does that have to do with anything?"

She shrugged. "Probably not much, except it proves the Fistians know a thing or two. Mostly I'm just curious. I'd venture the guess that they changed the physical characteristics of the rare earth radioactive elements in your body, making them harmless? That's a cute trick. The miners would be happy if they performed it with the radioactive deposits so they would be easier to mine."

"Many rare earths aren't radioactive," I said, "so yeah, the miners are interested in those and would be happy if the Fistians made the others safe. But that would only makes things worse. We want to make it harder for them, not easier."

"Oh. Scratch that idea then." She looked disappointed.

"Just a sec," said Lars. "Let's go the other way, shall we? Suppose Fistians can make all the rare earths on the planet radioactive?"

"Assuming they could do that," I said, "they wouldn't. They want to continue living here. It's their home. What you suggest is the same thing as poisoning a village's water supply all over Hard Fist. That's not a viable solution or moral action."

Lars put his palms on the table and pushed himself half-erect. He looked very tired, more tired than I was. "I think we're done here then. I see no solution. We might want to start thinking about abandoning our work and prepare to leave Hard Fist. I hate to leave work unfinished, but we might be forced to do so, and better sooner than later."

***

I slept for twelve hours and awoke to the news that miners from Middle Finger had marched on Marcello's village only to encounter the defensive shield. They fired upon it, wasting a lot of ammo. Frustrated, they returned to Middle Finger to look for heavier artillery. I immediately thought of the explosives they often used to uncover a new vein of ore.

"That large a self-sustaining shield is beyond our technology," said Dad2 as he served me a substantial breakfast. "It would be interesting to know how they do it."

Yeah, another mystery. The Fistians didn't have a lot of starship drives sitting around they could use power sources.

Thinking of the ancestors, I said, "I'm not sure many Fistians know how it's done. They're an extreme case of a post-technological civilization, meaning, in their case, that they now have different priorities and are just users of old technology. They're like nuns and monks in Earth monasteries during the early spaceflight era, eschewing technology to be one with their planet, but using cell phones when they had to do so. Except all the Fistians are like that, and Hard Fist is their monastery."

"Interesting observation," Dad2 said, sitting across from me. "And I'm glad you haven't forgotten your history lessons. Or your exosociology thesis."

"You're right. I'm more interested in Fistian history and its connections to their present culture. They stood up to the Marauders and paid a huge price, but they were able to keep their planet, so they revere it. They have plenty of practice battling invaders, though. I think they would have given the Tali a run for their money."

"Curious expression, that. The Tali thought Humans and Rangers were just vermin, but they soon learned otherwise. They were lucky we convinced Swarm not to eliminate them. Are we the Tali to the Fistians?"

"Maybe to some, although their hatred for Marauders goes beyond what we felt for Tali because the Marauders were a lot worse. But every threatening step the miners take reinforces the Fistians' idea that we are the Marauders returning to finish the job they started."

"I wish we could do something," Dad2 said.

"We can. First, we need some protection. Then you and I have to visit Middle Finger."

"You can't carry guns into Middle Finger."

"The protection I'm talking about doesn't come from guns. The Fistians will provide it."

I knew I was being optimistic about getting it from the ancestors, though. First, could they provide it? Second, would they want to do so? My plan counted on their help. If I didn't get it, I might be first in line to board a ship fleeing Hard Fist.

***

I'm sure the Fistians wouldn't have let Dad2 into their village alone, but we were admitted together after a bit of negotiation. That shield opened up long enough to let us squeeze in so we could negotiate.

"I want to apologize for the behavior of my people," Dad2 said to Mama Dora after a deep bow of respect. "And also thank you for saving my daughter's life."

"You aren't here only for that," she said. I'd known she would be cautious. And the Fistians had no reason to negotiate: Hard Fist belonged to them. We were just guests. Mama Dora had seen through our ruse. *Will that matter?*

"We need to ask an immense favor," I said. "I have a plan to put an end to hostilities. Or at least get the miners to think about ending them."

"I understand that there has been much talk between Brainsville scientists and Middle Finger miners. Without our participation, I might add." I digested that. *Another faux pas?* We had showed no respect for Fistian opinions. "Will more talk do any good? We don't trust the miners anymore."

"I understand your reluctance. And you're completely justified. Most Human scientists no longer trust the miners either, but we are in the minority among Humans on this planet. You let my father and me into your village. We expect a different greeting in Middle Finger. That's where you can help."

I made my request.

"I consider you a Fistian, Asako," said Mama Dora. She studied Dad2. "Can we also trust you, Kobayashi Father of the First Born Asako?"

He shrugged and smiled. "Trust must begin somewhere. You have no reason to trust me, but I am Asako's father. Her only one now. I can't let her do this alone."

Mama Dora thought a moment with head down while swatting away flies in the intense heat with her tail and pawing the earth a bit. I didn't envy her. She had to make a decision that might negatively affect all her people, not just those in her village. Normally she would probably consult with Fistian elders and possibly the ancestors. I'd argued that we didn't have time to do that, and the last consultation could be carried out in the caverns. The ancestors didn't have to go along with my plan, after all, even if live Fistians wanted them to. Or they couldn't because they didn't have the means. And, if the ancestors didn't go along, the live Fistians wouldn't either.

"I'll call Marcello then. He will guide you to the grotto."

Chapter Twenty-Nine

I was able to study the caverns in more detail this time. I saw my father's jaw drop several times, beginning with his rubbing of the luminescent moss on the walls. When we entered the room of urns, he stopped, mesmerized by the scene. It was almost a new physical experience for me too, but it was accompanied this time by many pleasant memories, except for those involving the Marauders, which were horrible.

Each urn glowed softly. Rows and rows of them, some on many ledges, others on the rocky floor. They also flickered as if an old-fashioned wax candle were inside, making the shadows dance around the cavern. The soft music wafted in the breeze that originated from deeper within the cave. There seemed to be magic in that ancient repository of minds, but it wasn't really magic, only a magical experience. I now knew some ancestors as persons who had once lived and now dispensed their wisdom among living Fistians. I felt like a Fistian, and I was proud.

"I-I can't count them all," Dad2 said in a whisper.

"Marcello tells me there are many more here and around the planet," I said. "The ones here are the oldest, dating back to when they discovered the technology."

"That must be an enormous number. I mean, for the whole planet."

"Not really. Fistians live a long time."

"And they don't use anti-senescent drugs." Dad2 seemed deep in thought. "We have people who would love to study this."

"Not possible," said Marcello. "These are our ancestors. We can't have Humans desecrating these sites."

"But we're here."

"Asako became a Fistian here. She can come anytime she wants if she can remember the way. If you survive the experience, you will also be a Fistian. Be forewarned. Some of our own young don't survive it."

I considered that. "I'd forgotten there is a danger," I said. I glanced at Dad2, then back at Marcello. "Is this really necessary?"

"If we are to trust your father completely. And there's always a danger. Not a physical danger, but a mental one. Some minds cannot accept the invasion. We had to bring you here to save your life, so we were willing to take the risk. With the radiation cure, you were already halfway a Fistian anyway. And without that cure, you would have died. I don't know if our shaman could have packed your essence into an urn, though."

"Dad2, maybe you'd better wait outside."

My father looked annoyed. "You heard what Marcello said. And I must accompany you to Middle Finger. I can't send you there alone, and Marcello clearly can't accompany you. He'd be shot on sight."

"That's all true," said Marcello. "I certainly couldn't accompany your daughter, not after leading the war party there and planting the spear at Macar's feet. And you can't go alone either, thinking that would protect Asako. It would be much too dangerous without our help." The flickering glow of some urns brightened into a white light. "They are ready."

Again Marcello made a circle with those particular urns, and we went into its center.

"We are ready, Asako," said the voices in my head. I nodded and smiled at Dad2.

I became the eyes for the voices as my father slapped hands to his ears and sank to his knees.

"Be gentle," I said to the ancestors.

***

Middle Finger didn't have a shield, so Dad2 and I just marched into the mining camp like we belonged there. Our first confrontation was with a teenage boy, older than Natasha, who unleashed his pet to attack us. Our personal shields, provided by the ancestors, sizzled. The pet ran away howling. The boy scampered away too.

"That was a nice touch," I said. "You didn't have that added personal zap at the village, did you?"

"Maybe they figure it's more useful for a personal shield," Dad2 said.

The idea about personal shields had been percolating for a while in my mind until it finally took form while talking with the ancestors: the only way I could venture into the miners' camp was to have some protection. I wasn't a gun person; neither was Dad2. But I remembered Doc's telling me SEB ships didn't carry offensive weapons, only shields. While I didn't believe the miners would attack me, knowing Dad2 and I were protected allowed me to be comfortable trying a bit of diplomacy backed up by technology. If we didn't succeed, leaving Hard Fist would then be analogous to an SEB ship fleeing a violent solar system.

When the ancestor-scientists described how to miniaturize the villagers' shields to something portable and wearable, I was only a conduit for recording the info on my wi-fi implant. I couldn't have made sense of it, being neither a physicist nor engineer, but we had people in Brainsville who could.

Unlike the design used in starships, the Fistian design was scalable and needed no hull to support it, only the ground. I'd guessed that scalability property because all villages were a bit different depending on the local topography. I'd remembered that helicopter ride with Dad2 and the trip to Drell's village had shown the apparent uniformity gave way to local adaptations. Of course, that was a gamble, but it was one that I'd won.

"What was that animal that tried to attack us?" I said.

"That was an Earth animal called a dog. They were called Human's best friend and developed into different varieties as ancient Humans discovered agriculture and began living in groups larger than tribes."

I should have known more about Humans' prehistory. "I'm surprised they survived the Tali invasion of Earth."

"That brutal remaking of our home planet into a copy of the Tali home world wasn't completely successful. There were Humans who survived too, enough to mount a resistance that lasted many years. But Earth is still less developed than other worlds and minus much of its original flora and fauna."

I nodded. I knew some of that history, but I'd forgotten about Humans' pets. I guessed they didn't often appear in history books. I remembered something called a wolf, though. *Maybe dogs are related to wolves?*

"I always wondered when I was studying on Sanctuary why Humans picked that planet when there are so many like Earth that are more appropriate for Humans to live on."

"I don't know. Something else to learn. My forte isn't history, you know." Dad2 looked around. "Where is everyone?"

A mob, led by Boris Macar, rounded a corner as if to answer my father's question. They didn't look happy to see us.

***

"Well, if it isn't the centaur-loving little brat and her treasonous father," said Macar. "You'll make some good hostages to force the rest of the scientists to get in line with the program."

"You can't harm us or take us hostage," Dad2 said. "We only want to talk. If you refuse, we'll be on our way."

"For a genius, you sure can spout stupidity," said Macar. "Grab'em, men!"

Six miners tried to grab us. They suffered the dog's fate, but they didn't run away; their hands and arms continued to shake from the zaps.

"Who's stupid now?" I said. "We borrowed a bit of Fistian technology. If they can provide us with personal shields, do you think they'll care about your puny weapons?" I saw Macar turn pale. "I don't care if you folks want to commit suicide, but I'd think you'd like to discuss your plans first with us to see if there are reasonable alternatives."

Macar shrugged. "Sure, some more talk can't hurt, I guess. We'll have a community meeting. Follow us to the big tent."

Item #2 was now checked off from my agenda. #1 had been the personal shields, something generated from a little black box that hung from our belts. Brainsville technicians had cobbled them together from designs provided by the ancestors. Only the ancestors knew how they worked or even what the energy source was. I'm no techie, but I guessed it fed off quantum zero-point energy just like our stardrives. I didn't doubt that some

Humans in Brainsville would now be busy trying to reverse-engineer them to get at the underlying science, but that might take years, proving what I said to the miners was true: They were up against a smart foe in the Fistians.

***

Daniel Chang took a seat next to us. A dozen miners had joined us around a large circular meeting table. Outside that circle, many others had taken seats, but many were standing too. In spite of the shields, I felt a bit vulnerable. This was a hostile environment, and it made me nervous. I glanced at Dad2; he smiled back, which assured me that item #3 was proceeding as planned.

"I don't know how you two pulled it off," Daniel said in a whisper, "but congratulations on getting them to talk. I'm still not convinced that Fistians would have an easy time of it, by the way, but I'd rather avoid hostilities. That can accomplish nothing."

The despotic Macar had taken over Daniel's role. He was a bit pompous about pounding a gavel on the table, but that was probably meant more to silence the noisy miners, some of them still hearing for the first time about our shields.

"OK, let's hear it, you two," sai Macar. "What kind of deal are you offering?"

"Did I imply that Fistians want to make a deal?" Dad2 said. "That's not the case." Angry mumblings greeted that statement. Macar didn't look happy either. "We're the ones who want to make a deal between them and you that will avoid many Human casualties. The scientists only want peace so we can carry on our research. Your motivation should be a bit more fundamental: You'll want to make peace with Fistians if you want to continue to live."

"Consorting with the enemy and relaying their threats isn't going to lead to peace."

"If they want a fight, we'll give it to them!" said another miner in back of us.

I turned. "That kind of attitude will get you all killed," I said. "Believe me, you don't understand who you're dealing with. You might have come from your home planets in starships, but it's naïve of you to think you're technologically superior to Fistians."

"They're just a bunch of agrarian savages," said Macar. "They had no idea what they had here on Hard Fist. We're somebody who did, so we're taking it. That's how life works. The strongest survive."

"Despite reservations of many Fistians," I said, "their leaders allowed Human scientists to come here and then you miners. Neither group has gone out of their way to understand them. Or thank them, for that matter."

"Nothing to understand!" said Macar, glaring at me. "ITUIP has given us carte blanche to mine as much of this swampy hell as we want. And we bust our butts doing it, so we've earned our rewards. We won't let them take that away."

"Stop it!" That was a scream from a small voice. I turned to see a young girl, her braids bouncing behind her back, approach me from behind. "This is crazy. You're all lazy, greedy old men who will go to war with a noble people just to make your mining operations easier and increase your production. You have the whole planet to mine. And you don't have to destroy it or its people in doing it!"

"Shut your brat up!" said another miner to Macar.

He pounded his gavel and glared at the vocal miner. "You shut up! Let's listen to what she has to say." He gestured toward his daughter. "Go on, Natasha."

"A Fistian named Marcello saved my life, along with Asako," she said. "Doesn't that mean anything to you idiots? I think they're special, and we should learn from them. We'll be better off being their friends than their enemies. But you can't get that into your thick skulls. You're all dirty old men who don't have one ounce of brains!"

She turned and ran from the meeting tent crying.

Pandemonium ensued. That was #3 on my list: make the miners understand. Natasha had accomplished that point, not me.

Chapter Thirty

Natasha's outburst succeeded where Dad2 and I had been fast approaching a roadblock. Things changed for the better a lot faster than I could have imagined. It took no time at all, it seemed, before Fistians began to sell produce and other goods in the mining camps. Miners and their families, what few had come to Hard Fist already, often could be found mingling with Fistians there and in Fistian villages where shields had come down. There was a new spirit of collaboration, with Fistians working with scientists in Brainsville and miners all over the planet, adopting mining techniques the Fistians knew that didn't damage the environment.

I was embarrassed. While I could argue that challenging the miners was a catalyst for Natasha, that little girl had been the real hero. It had taken a lot of spunk to tell off that group of gruff old miners, her father included. Maybe especially her father. Natasha and I were drawn to each other and bonded like two sisters.

Of course, Marcello was a hero too. If he hadn't saved Natasha, Hard Fist's future could have been entirely different. I told him so when he sauntered into the ancestors' grotto with Natasha on his back. He helped her down. She stood with hands on hips and faced me.

"We saw a drooler, Asako!" she said.

She was clearly excited by the experience and breathing heavily. I hoped it hadn't brought back painful memories. Of course, being out of breath could occur from just riding Marcello full speed through Hard Fist's rainforests. *But is Marcello taking chances with her?*

"Not up close, I hope."

She shook her head. "Ooh. I never want to be that close to one again. What's the agenda for today?"

I smiled. She was precocious. Reminded me of someone. Couldn't imagine how she could be Macar's daughter, but there she was with hands on hips and ready for action.

"I'm going to try to learn more about Marauders," I said. "You'd better wait outside with Marcello." She made a face. "Don't worry. Your day will come."

"Asako will be safe," said Marcello. "Let's see if we can find the berries Mama Dora gave Asako the first time. Just in case."

I had promised Mama Dora not to pry into any technological secrets the ancestors possessed. I accepted her warning that perhaps Humans weren't ready for them. Considering Fistians thought Humans were better off without them, it seemed natural for me to heed that advice. I was sure that the ancestors understood FTL travel and how we flitted around near-Earth planets by hopping among metaverses, so I didn't have much to offer them in return anyway, beyond a few gizmos Fistians had no use for.

One of the secrets we almost had was the personal shield, though. Engineers were still trying to reverse engineer it because it could be useful for SEB's exploration of far-out solar systems. I imagined it would take them a few years. And I also know that Fistians considered that a trifle, something like those beads European explorers gave to Native Americans so long ago. There were certain parallels to that history. Those Native American cultures often had known more about astronomy, telling time, and navigation than the European invaders. I hoped it would take a long time to reverse engineer the personal shield.

The Fistians were also being coy about letting Humans interact with the ancestors. I couldn't blame them. And that Fistian policy seemed to humble a lot of Humans who needed humbling!

The Marauders still intrigued me. Were they off somewhere, lurking and ready to pounce on any galactic civilization that dared enter their territory? A fear of them—maybe mixed with respect—seemed to be an integral part of Fistian culture. Humans and Rangers had suffered from the Tali's excesses, and many Humans still held a grudge against them, but Fistians' paranoia toward Marauders seemed to go far beyond grudges. *Who are the Marauders?*

***

"Seems like a lot of progress has been made," said Shallow Swimmer, the Ranger SEB captain of the next ITUIP exploratory vessel to visit Hard Fist.

A shuttle had left the starship in orbit and landed near Mama Dora's village. The research for my thesis wasn't done yet, so I wouldn't be leaving with our visitors, but Shallow Swimmer had another agenda, the miners' petition to join ITUIP.

I nodded to Mama Dora, Lars Swenson, and Daniel Chang, who had cleaned up a bit for the meeting in the Fistian village.

"We resolved some differences," said Mama Dora. She towered over the small captain who perched on a dais her Tali XO had set up for her. The Fistian clan mother even dwarfed the Tali who was much larger than a normal Human. I saw some furtive glances from Mama Dora toward the Tali—he did look more like Marauder than Human, but within that black leathery face she couldn't detect any beak...and he didn't have one.

The Rangers had been Humans' partners for a long time. Their common enemy, the Tali, and the goal to populate New Haven bonded Humans and Rangers forever. They differed more from Humans than Fistians did, though, while the Tali, my original and wrong candidates for being the Marauders, were more similar. That just shows that it's the cultural and mental makeup of a people that's important, not their appearances. And you often can't understand actions without knowing the reasons for those actions.

Lars and Daniel nodded. "We'd like to speed up the application for ITUIP membership," said Daniel.

"I don't see any problem with that, considering what we've seen," said Shallow Swimmer. "The only thing we noted was that the Human miners need to clean up their act a bit. This planet is pristine compared to many. We want to keep it that way, right?" Rangers were the leaders in near-Earth space in maintaining pristine ecospheres.

The different representatives assented according to their manner, something the AI would have a hard time expressing.

Shallow Swimmer's ship's AI had handed over communications to Brainsville's Einstein, but the translation from the Rangers' strange language, buzzspeak, still came over loud and clear, drowning out the low volume buzz. The tentacles around her mouth excitedly indicated all points of the compass, a gesture intended to include all of Hard Fist.

"Correct," said Daniel, who had decided to vocalize the assent, I guess. "We're working with Fistians on that. Turns out they know a lot about mining technologies that won't damage the environment. It adds a bit to the cost, but we want to keep the place livable for our kids too."

I smiled. Natasha Macar was responsible for educating miners. Maybe my acolyte—I liked to call her that now, although she was like a sister—could have a career as an interstellar diplomat. Right now, though, she wanted to be just like me and study Fistians. I didn't know if there would be room for two Fistian experts in the galaxy, but what the heck?

"We need to know more about this ITUIP," said Mama Dora, "but it sounds like joining your federation could be beneficial for everyone here on Hard Fist. Just seeing a starship captain who isn't Human indicates an understanding and openness all Fistians can admire."

I nodded. My dream for Hard Fist was becoming a reality.

Epilogue

A year later, the crew of another ITUIP starship waited for me as I said my goodbyes to my parents, Mama Dora, Marcello, and Natasha. I gave Marcello the longest hug.

"I'll be back soon," I whispered into his ear.

"Natasha will continue your work," he said, whispering back. He stepped away from me and saluted. "You'll come back as Dr. Kobayashi Number Two. Don't let it go to your head."

"Never. And don't get spoiled with that lightweight punk riding you."

"She's growing too, and she'll keep me exercising. I bet you'll gain weight on Sanctuary. There isn't much space there to run around in."

Marcello had visited Sanctuary for three standard weeks to learn about hydroponics. That knowledge would be useful to some Fistians—he was included in that group—who wanted to expand to desert regions of Hard Fist and to other places in their solar system.

I nodded at a shy Fistian on the edge of the little crowd who was watching our goodbye hugs. "Is she the one?"

His eyebrows danced. "Maybe. Mama Dora thinks so."

"What do the ancestors in the urns say?"

"I don't care. That's none of their business anyway."

Another fact for my thesis: not all Fistians sought the ancestors' approval for their mates, although I knew some did. Clan mothers like Mother Dora were the ancestors' representatives anyway, and their approval was what counted.

***

I didn't want to contradict Marcello's ideas about what might become of Natasha. Yes, she had already been a big help obtaining data for my thesis, but I'd learned some things about her that made her contributions already special. I'd seen someone who could become a gifted musician like Denise.

Natasha had perfect pitch and could keep track of nuanced and complicated rhythms. I'd even spoken to her father about her gifts.

"It's not practical to become a musician," he'd said. "She should become a miner's wife and have lots of children."

I'd controlled myself and thought of a more diplomatic response.

"She could do that, but that miner's gain might be the galaxy's loss. Can you at least let her choose her own future?"

Macar shrugged. "I suppose. What makes you think she won't choose to be a miner's wife?"

"She might. She might choose to do something we can't even imagine now. But let her develop her musical talent."

"Not much chance of that on Hard Fist!"

I thought a moment. "Maybe there is. The Fistians are very musical. Can she help me catalog some of their music for my thesis?"

"I've never seen anyone so obsessed with a bunch of—" He caught himself, looked flustered, and then continued. "—ETs." He looked at the top of his tent. "How's that going to develop her musical talent? She has a flute and guitar right here. Everything she plays is very soothing for me after a hard day's work."

I nodded. "Listening to the Fistians, she'll develop other ideas. And, who knows, some Fistian might want flute or guitar lessons?"

Macar smiled. "I guess that's OK, as long as you're around to protect her."

I bit my tongue again. "From whom?"

"She still explores a lot. There are droolers about, and who knows what else?"

Not the answer I'd expected. "A deal then?"

"Sure. Whatever she wants."

I was beginning to like the burly miner....

***

Natasha couldn't help me with one item for my thesis research that still remained a mystery: the Marauders. None of the Fistians could—the live ones didn't know any more than the ancestors. I had a good idea what they looked like from the latter. But no one seemed to know where they were.

Even the famous shipbuilders, who used to live in the Nexus and played an important role in Human and near-Earth history, hadn't been so reclusive. They seemed to be the spokespeople for Swarm now, and they were still a bit aloof and not willing participants in ITUIP affairs. If I ever met one, I would ask her or him if they knew about the Marauders, but for now that question would remain unanswered.

From what I'd learned about the Marauders, they wouldn't like any of the intelligent lifeforms in near-Earth space and beyond. I hoped we'd never meet them. Maybe they would wage war on all of us, including the shipbuilders and Swarm? Would we then have to allow

Swarm to intercede then and wipe out all traces of the Marauders? I'd never want to make that decision!

***

I gave my parents one last hug and entered the shuttle.

Did I say the SEB ship was the *Balboa*? Doc was still an intern on that starship that waited for me in orbit. The trip to Sanctuary could be interesting.

I hadn't had the dyad v. triad talk with Mom or Dad2 yet, and maybe never would. Most people just bounced around a bit at first, trying one or the other or staying a monad, so I wasn't in a hurry. I'd always thought that lack of that talk stemmed from my parents' confusion: they couldn't quite decide whether I was an adult and a peer, or just a little kid who happened to be their daughter. They knew about Doc, of course, but did they remember he was on the *Balboa*?

Thought it didn't matter. I'd soon return. Maybe I'd have that talk with Mom. I didn't know enough about her choices, so she could provide some useful information about relationships. Of course, I didn't even know if I wanted a dyadic one! Anything beyond a monad could be restrictive. *I'm pretty independent!* And there was that introspective debate I'd had with myself on that beach in Nirvana while being lazy in Doc's arms.

I did know it was time to finish writing and defend my thesis. *Will I pass?* It didn't matter. I would still be this part of the galaxy's leading authority on Fistian culture! Would I work something out with Doc? And add a Doc2? Maybe, or Doc and I would just become great friends.

It would be a great adventure to see what my future would bring.

Note from A. B.:

You have just finished *The Secret of the Urns*. I hope you enjoyed it. I recognize you have many books to choose from for your reading; I'm humbled and honored you chose mine and thank you for doing so. Please write a review on Amazon for this book if at all possible. That would help other readers who might wonder what the book is like, and it would provide me with some interesting feedback. Thank you for being a reader. If you are a young reader, you can still write that review with your parents' help. And tell your friends and relatives about the book too.

The Secret Lab is another sci-fi mystery in this young-adult series you might enjoy. It's set in the same fictional universe, but at an earlier time.

And don't miss other sci-fi from my American friend, Steven M. Moore. *The Chaos Chronicles Trilogy Collection*, for example, bundles together three novels and will take you from a dystopian Earth dominated by multinationals and controlled by their mercenaries, to the first star colonies and first contact and beyond. It is also set in this same fictional universe.

Note that neither Steve nor I give away our novels (his are sometimes on sale at Smashwords, though), but we do give away our short fiction. See the blog categories "Steve's Shorts," "ABC Shorts," and the list of free PDFs free on the webpage "Free Stuff & Contests" at Steve's website, http://stevenmmoore.com. We can't publish everything we write, even the good stuff (the bad stuff never sees the light of day, of course). Steve's website also contains much more information about us and our books.

In libris libertas!

A.B. CAROLAN

Notes, Disclaimers, and Acknowledgments

This sci-fi mystery for young adults and adults young-at-heart, like *The Secret Lab*, focuses on scientific ethics and cultural destruction. While my first novel (really the second edition of Steven M. Moore's *The Secret Lab* rewritten and reedited by yours truly) deals with the potential perils of cloning and genetic manipulation but also features the genial cat Mr. Paws, who couldn't have existed without it, this novel treats bullying, discrimination, and xenophobia, here by Humans against native Fistians. Things get twisted around as Humans on Hard Fist realize that their arrogance and hubris aren't logically supportable.

Nevertheless, this is a mystery—perhaps a bit strange in the sci-fi context, but still a mystery. Mysteries aren't new to sci-fi, of course. Our two favorites are Asimov's *Caves of Steel* and *The Naked Sun*. *The Secret Lab* also was a mystery because the Fearsome Four were trying to figure out Mr. Paws's origin. Here Asako tries to understand how Fistains use their ancestors to preserve Fistian culture.

Most of the first three chapters of this novel appeared in 2007 as one of Mr. Moore's short stories titled "Marcello and Me" (it was included in his short story collection, *Pasodobles in a Quantum Stringscape* in 2013). That story, this one, *The Secret Lab*, Mr. Moore's *Rogue Planet*, and all the Dr. Carlos stories (I contributed one of those) are set in the same fictional universe as his "Chaos

Chronicles Trilogy," which, among many other things, shows how the ITUIP (International Trade Union of Independent Planets) grew to be a political force among the near-Earth planets. (That trilogy is now bundled together as *The Chaos Chronicles Trilogy Collection* and is to Mr. Moore's oeuvre as the Foundation Trilogy is to Mr. Asimov's.) The short story, though, won a prize, and it's a lot of fun, so I coaxed Mr. Moore into letting me write a complete novel based on it.

The Rangers and Tali, other near-Earth peoples, first appeared in Mr. Moore's *Sing a Zamba Galactica*, the second novel in the "Chaos Chronicles Trilogy," while the story of how the Rangers ended up on New Haven before Humans, "Flight from the Mother World," also appeared in *Pasodobles in a a Quantum Stringscape*. That strange collective mind, Swarm, played an important role in *Sing a Zamba Galactica* and *Come Dance a Cumbia...with Stars in Your Hand!*, books two and three in the "Chaos Chronicles Trilogy," where other Humans meet even more ET cultures. With Fistians, near-Earth space is becoming crowded! (I added some new ETs in my short story "Caitlin O'Riley," found in Mr. Moore's blog category "ABC Shorts").

The short story "Marcello and Me" owes its origins to a series of what-ifs and experiences in Mr. Moore's life. Growing up in the diverse state of California, he was sheltered from xenophobic experiences by parents who wanted nothing to do with discrimination. Their best friends were Armenians, so he heard about the Armenian genocide perpetrated by the Turks secondhand, and about the Japanese internment camps during the war, but he only experienced America's racism in the flesh when he visited the San Joaquin Valley's migrant camps with his mother and went east and saw it in Maryland and

Virginia, and much later in "liberal" Boston. He was exposed to Native American culture in Colombia (mostly the Sibundoy tribe), and that experience probably influenced this story the most and gave me some great ideas too—we often talked about Steve's English professor N. Scott Momaday, Pulitzer Prize winner for *House Made of Dawn*, and Steve's idea for including Native American references in his new post-apocalyptic thriller *The Last Humans*. Fistian reverence for their ancestors is less mystical and more technologically based, though.

The story contains two different themes: ignorance spawns xenophobic and bigoted behavior, and different and ancient cultures might surprise you with what they knew ages before ours. We have seen both themes play out here on Earth! Many Native American cultures were more advanced in agricultural and astronomical methods than their white invaders, for example. Arabs invented algebra (as the name indicates), and Arabs and Chinese were great astronomers too.

Here there's tragedy: Fistians' historical cycles of cultural ups and downs left them with only the ancestors' memories (note that I didn't say "ancestral memories"). That tragedy turns out to be a powerful lesson. Whether that resonates with you or not, it makes for a good story, so I told it, with Mr. Moore's permission…and encouragement. If I failed to do Fistians justice in the telling, I apologize. I assume Marcello, Mama Dora, and all their relatives and friends will forgive me.

As usual, many people helped to prepare this book for publication. I called on many of Steve's friends to help me: Donna Carrick, a wonderful lady and talented author in her own right, runs Carrick Publishing and does a marvelous job with formatting; Sara Carrick keeps coming up with great cover ideas; Carol Shetler and Scott

Dyson were beta-readers who not only find errors in logic but catch any left-over copy editing errors; and Amanda Kerr of BookBuzz will do her fine job on advertising the launch of this book. Steve counts them all as friends; so do I.

A. B. Carolan
Donegal, Ireland
July, 2018

About the Author

A. B. Carolan is rumored to be a descendant of the great Irish harpist and songwriter Turlough O'Carolan. Whether true or not, people say he was a child who was stolen and raised by leprechauns. He now lives in Donegal, Ireland, where he communicates frequently with his American friend and collaborator, Steven M. Moore.

A.B. CAROLAN